HOLIDAY FOR MURDER

The rakish star of a small-town musical is murdered—and Kenworthy is the only one who can find out why . . .

"Satisfying and plausible . . . An unexpectedly dramatic climax!"   —Publishers Weekly

LESSON IN MURDER

A teacher is publicly accused of wrongdoing by four female students—and then found murdered. The Inspector's assignment: find out whodunnit—and why . . .

"Penetrating glances into the adolescent mind . . ."
                                                              —Kirkus Reviews

DEAD MAN'S PATH

Who *didn't* have a motive to kill Edward Barson? The suspects are many but the clues are few as Kenworthy tries to solve a big mystery in a small town . . .

"Top-notch!"   —Library Journal

TWICE DEAD

A sixteen-year-old schoolgirl and her teacher disappear—and soon the missing-persons case turns to murder . . .

"Read Hilton . . . and you'll wind up a fan!"
                                                              —Anniston Star

continued on next page

RANSOM GAME

The kidnappers made a strange demand: let an imprisoned man raise white mice in his cell. But the Inspector has a feeling it's more than just a bizarre prank . . .

"Hilton will hold readers hostage with this one!"
—Chicago Sun-Times

FOCUS ON CRIME

A prominent pastor is found dead—and Kenworthy tries to discover who committed the sinful deed . . .

"Hilton tells the story with an artistry that transfixes the reader."
—Publishers Weekly

CORRIDORS OF GUILT

A gang of football hooligans, a clever crossword buff, and an obscure government agency are the ingredients in a puzzling case of murder . . .

"One of veteran Hilton's most distinctive concoctions."
—Kirkus Reviews

TARGET OF SUSPICION

A man is shot dead on an army battle range—an accident or murder? Kenworthy aims to hit the bull's-eye of truth . . .

"A great character!"
—Birmingham Post (England)

MORE MYSTERIES FROM THE
BERKLEY PUBLISHING GROUP . . .

DEATH IN MIDWINTER

JOHN BUXTON HILTON

BERKLEY PRIME CRIME, NEW YORK

This Berkley Prime Crime Book contains the complete text of the original hardcover edition.
It has been completely reset in a typeface designed for easy reading, and was printed from new film.

DEATH IN MIDWINTER

A Berkley Prime Crime Book / published by arrangement with the Estate of John Buxton Hilton

PRINTING HISTORY
Cassell & Company edition published 1969
Berkley Prime Crime edition / May 1994

ISBN: 0-425-14224-8

Berkley Prime Crime Books are published by The Berkley Publishing Group, 200 Madison Avenue, New York, NY 10016.
The name BERKLEY PRIME CRIME and the BERKLEY PRIME CRIME design are trademarks of Berkley Publishing Corporation.

PRINTED IN THE UNITED STATES OF AMERICA

10 9 8 7 6 5 4 3 2 1

For Anna

◆ 1 ◆

IN A STONE farmhouse in a Pennine valley an old man lay dying. At a Whitehall desk a new young Parliamentary Secretary allowed himself a moment's admiration for his signature, appended for the first time in his life to a Statutory Instrument. In New Scotland Yard a detective superintendent sucked at a pipe too choked to draw properly and swore wearily to his sergeant.

"Shiner, I'd rather be a humble rozzer."

It was Boxing Day, and Simon Kenworthy had spent it in a welter of paper and telephones, at the centre of a massive metropolitan web. Not once since a 999 call had sparked off the case had he exchanged words with anyone outside the office.

"To think that I joined this lot because I wanted a job where I could meet people."

And two hundred miles away an old man whom he had never met was nearing his natural end. It was a wild, primeval night as Kenworthy eventually came to reconstruct it, a bleak back-cloth for a man who had no desire to meet his Maker.

Carrion Clough lay in a splash of lunar shadow. When the moon emerged occasionally from the scud, the silhouette of a dry-stone wall sloped jaggedly away down the moor. Beyond lay patches of sere bracken and dead heather, rippling like surf when the moon shone.

Tommy Booth leaned his elbows on the uneven coping of the wall and looked northwest across the water. A cutting wind from the east was ruffling the reservoir. The air whined in telephone wires, with an endless descant from the dozens of rills that ran down into the flooded valley.

Tommy's world was never empty, even though he spent most of his time alone. He had once seen the weathercock on St. Lawrence's spire rising from the waves, and that was after a wet autumn and the melting snows of a heavy winter, when it was not there to be seen. Many other men had seen the ancient steeple, but only in summer droughts, when the waters receded thirty feet down the tumbled grit-stone of the shore. On such occasions Tommy not only saw with others the wrecked walls and yawning gables of the submerged village; he heard the peal from the belfry and the crowing of the cock in old Abraham Drabble's yard.

Tonight he saw a Crimean sergeant of the Grenadiers striding purposefully up the silver lane that climbed to the brow of Moss Hill.

It may be that the soldier was not dressed and equipped in the precise parade-ground fashion of his age and regiment, but he had all the accoutrements that Tommy had once seen sketched in an Edwardian school primer: white cross-straps and a square-cut, pipe-clayed pack, a scarlet tunic and a bearskin, with a musket at the short trail, which he transferred gallantly to the slope as he turned up the sheep-track that would lead him home. It was nearly a hundred years since Sergeant Thomas Halliwell had died, and Tommy Booth was only thirty-nine; but history fascinated him, and he lived on terms of reckless intimacy with such of it as had come to his knowledge.

He was unmoved by the apparition. He waited until the ram-rod figure had vanished behind a lip of rising ground, then he turned slowly and made his way down the lane towards the Legless Volunteer. When he reached a point from which he could see Moss Farm, he turned and looked back at the pale lighted window behind which Thomas John was dying.

Thomas John was dying, it was common knowledge in the Clough, and Thomas John's father had come back from Sebastopol with his musket on his shoulder. To Tommy Booth it was unquestionably normal.

Behind the pale lighted window Margaret Halliwell turned down the wick of the oil-lamp, which was beginning to smoke, and carried it from the table to the tall chest-of-drawers. As she moved across the room, the light shifted over her grandfather's face, drawing a series of suggestive shadows, so that the features seemed to change from avarice to mephistophelian humour, from gauntness even to a certain placid kindliness. She stood still for a moment and looked at him. A breath sharper than usual jerked his body and threatened to wake him, but he slept on without moving his head on the pillow.

So it had been for three days. Time and again it had seemed that a breath would be his last, but always he had drawn himself back to life with some miraculous reserve. Now and then he had awakened, or, at least, had lain with his eyes open, cackling with the laughter of a gargoyle. Once he had taken off his woollen bed-cap because, he said, a parson had come into the room. Margaret did not know which parson he could imagine it to be. It must have been forty years ago, the story went, that he had picked up a curate in his arms and thrown him bodily over a five-foot wall into a slough of cattle stampings. Since then, parsons had stayed away from Moss Brow.

Margaret was not a stranger to death. She had seen her mother, in the bed that was now her own, when she had been taken in by her aunt Edith to lay her fourteen-year-old knuckles against the grey cheek.

"If you touch her, her memory won't haunt you, my poor pet."

She looked again at the old man—at the wooden handle hanging on a rope from the beam, so that he could pull himself up in bed—at the gnarled walking-stick between the bed and the wall, with which he had called her from downstairs thirty times a day for the last two years.

He stirred, sighed and opened his eyes.

"I want my pot," he said.

And when she had helped him to swing his legs over the bed, and had smoothed back his sheets, he spoke with unaffected sanity.

"Give me a grape."

It was as if he had wakened ordinarily from a nap on a summer's afternoon in the prime of his life. The wildness had gone from his eyes. Senility and decay had cleared from his brain for an inexplicable instant. He knew where he was. He knew Margaret. He knew about the grapes. And yet it was inconceivable that he could know about the grapes, which had been a Christmas present from the Penningtons. Margaret knew intuitively that he would die before midnight. She picked up the fruit-bowl.

Out in the lane Tommy Booth saw her shadow cross the window, and quickened his steps towards the inn.

It had been at the turn of the centuries—a decade and a half before Tommy was born—that the valley and its bleak village had been damned and inundated to ensure the water supply of a congeries of industrial towns some forty or fifty miles away. North of the water stretched the gathering grounds, from which every shepherd, every farmer, every cottager had had to go. It was only south of the reservoir, where the Moss Brow watershed drained away into the Cotter Brook, that a handful of habitations had been allowed to remain, together with a tiny school, shortly to be closed, and a single public house.

Tommy reached the forecourt of the Legless Volunteer, but he did not go in. Instead he stooped to peep through a corner of the tap-room window. Not seeing what he hoped for, he withdrew into an angle of the porch, thrust his hands deep into his trouser pockets and stood with his shoulder against the wall, the collar of his jacket turned up against the night air. He did not possess an overcoat.

For half an hour he stood thus, motionless, waiting for a ray of light to round a corner of the road. A bicycle approached, its dynamo humming against the rear tyre. The rider turned into the forecourt of the Volunteer and brought his machine to a standstill before dismounting, which he did by falling off sideways, with all the dignity of a marionette.

"Evening, Mr. Wilson."

The cyclist was a sparse, elderly man, in a Homburg hat and solid dark greatcoat, beneath which his bicycle clips looked cheaply incongruous.

"Hullo, Tommy. It's warmer inside, you know."

"I've nothing to lift the latch with tonight, Mr. Wilson."

"You never have, you crafty young devil. All right, then, come in. I'll lift the latch for you."

And he opened the door of the Volunteer, holding it for Tommy to precede him into the warm little bar. Four fatigued paper garlands spidered out into the corners from the low, age-blackened rafters. A large, hand-painted card on the counter wished customers Isaac and Martha Pennington's laboriously misspelt "Complements" of the season.

There were not many drinkers. The house had been a steady drain upon the brewers since the building of the dam, though they clung to its license out of some long-term global strategy. Four men were playing dominoes in a corner. Two were talking to the Penningtons. Wilson ordered two pints of mild beer and stuck the poker in the fire, for he always mulled his ale in winter. Tommy carried his latch-lifting pot to a small table near the window, apart from the others, a shabby, hungry figure, with yellow twisted teeth and a shapeless cloth cap, which he did not remove.

"Your health, Mr. Wilson."

"Cheers, Tommy."

Isaac Pennington wiped up smears with a grey dish-cloth.

"I don't know why you encourage him, Wilfred."

Ben Drabble, who did day-to-day maintenance jobs up at the dam, and who acted as water-bailiff when fly-fishers came up to the water's edge in season, asked how much he thought he had spent on Tommy in his life.

"I should say it averages a pint a night since we were in the Home Guard."

"Something like twenty years. Call it seven shillings a week, and that's an understatement. Eighteen pounds a year. As near as nothing three hundred and sixty pounds. And the rest."

Wilson laughed.

"I could have bought myself a car."

Wilson was the schoolmaster, who taught the Clough's dozen children without assistance, and had done so since the end of the First World War. At the same time he managed to stoke the school boiler, tend the not inconsiderable garden and deal in his antique, gracious cursive handwriting with the ever-increasing demand for administrative returns. He also advised Carrion Clough on everything from its income tax allowances to the latest racing form. Soon, his school was scheduled for closure. There would be a special bus to take the children into Cotter Bridge, and Wilfred Wilson, who had already been allowed to continue three years beyond the normal retiring age, was not sure whether the Committee would allow him to buy the abandoned school-house.

"Thomas John's sinking," he said, glad to change the subject away from his ludicrous generosity.

"So we shall have some visitors up the Clough," said Dick Haines, who kept the grocer's shop and sub-post office.

"Not they," Ben said. "There'll be none but young Margaret behind that coffin. Then she can go off and mourn for herself."

"They'll come. You'll see," Wilson told them. "Old Thomas John is worth a tidy penny."

"Let's hope he's told young Margaret where to look for it, then. It's not in the bank, you can bet. And there's no justice in the world if any of the others gets a brass button. It must be five years, if it's a day, since one of them came near here."

"Edith'll want her share. There was always plenty of the old man in that lass."

"That lad of hers is doing well."

"Anthony? Brightest boy I've ever met in my life, and I've met a few. He used to come here for his holidays, sometimes, before the war. You'll remember talking to him, Ben. I took him for a walk, over the Edge, when he'd have been about seven or eight. Talk? I couldn't get a word in edgeways, and when *I* say that, it means something. I showed him over some of the old barrows and Bronze Age bits and pieces. Damned if he didn't know more about them than I did."

Wilson drank deep.

"Member of the government now. Be in the cabinet before we know where we are. Seventeen or eighteen, he'd be, the last time he came here. But by then he'd no room for a decrepit old bugger like me."

Tommy Booth approached silently and placed his empty glass on the counter, ready to go out into the night, or drink another pint if somebody would buy him one. Wilson put a florin on the bar.

Then they all stopped talking. The outside door had opened and the jaded garlands were swaying in the draught. A strong, well-built woman in her late thirties came into the room, a woman with a complexion accustomed to rugged health and all weathers, but for the moment pale and a little dazed.

The landlord's wife leaned forward and spoke gently.

"Has he gone, love?"

"Half an hour ago. . . . Could I use your phone, please?"

"Come into the back room. I'll make you a hot drink. And I'll come back with you afterwards and help you to lay him out."

"I can manage," Margaret said.

The men were left alone.

"That's it, then," Ben said. "Now we shall see what we shall see. The old man always said he'd die one day, if he took it into his head. But he always swore they'd never bury him."

"He was a rum old stick."

"He said if God above commanded him, he'd go. But those that were left, he said, he'd never let them put him away."

Presently Martha Pennington returned alone to the bar.

"He asked her for a grape, and he said he wanted her to put one in his mouth and another in his hand, and she did that, and when she looked again, he'd gone. He died just like a baby, she says."

"I'll push my bike up to the farm with you when you go,"

Wilson said. "In case there's anything I can do. She's not thinking of spending another night up there alone, is she?"

"I wanted her to stay here and sleep, but she won't hear of it. She says if she came to no harm with him alive, she's sure she'll come to none with him dead."

"Aye. Stubborn as they come. Runs in the family. And it's a hard thing to say, but I think young Margaret's troubles are only just starting. We haven't heard the last of Thomas John yet, not by a long chalk. Keep a close eye on her, will you, Martha? And let me or the missus know if there's anything we can do. I'm not going to let the vultures get at Margaret Halliwell if I can help it."

Then the door opened again, and a fresh-faced young athlete with the Burma star among the ribbons on his policeman's tunic joined them.

"Evening, Jim. All the boggarts locked up for the night?"

The constable took off his helmet and put it on the counter. Isaac Pennington had already drawn him a pint.

"Thomas John's gone, Jim."

"I thought so. I followed young Margaret down. I should think the boggarts will be watching out for themselves, tonight. There was a damned old owl screeching down in the Plantation loud enough to make anyone believe in ghosts."

"Anything new in the big city, Jim?"

The constable recounted a variant on an old theme, a story about a medieval princess, an absent crusader and a chastity belt.

"If I lent you my Boccaccio, you wouldn't read him," Wilson said. "What luck with the gee-gees, that's more to the point? I haven't seen a paper or heard the news."

"Oh, you're all right on Porcelain Palace. Hundred to eight."

"Hope you remembered to put it on. Porcelain Palace—I won't tell you where I was when I had the inspiration."

• 2 •

SIMON KENWORTHY'S FACE was a study of pain, self-pity and a lingering remnant of disbelief as the convoy struggled up the snow-ridden wastes towards the gathering grounds.

"People *live* here," he said once, looking up at a sprawling stone farmstead, gripped in dune-edged drifts. But for the most part, he was silent, and Sergeant Wright did not disturb him in his misery.

Cotter Bridge had been bad enough: the hotel with dry horseradish sauce, caked in a lidless pot; the waitress with a cold—and the frustration of remaining weatherbound for three days, Carrion Clough being cut off by snow in all directions.

Wright knew by heart the meagre notes they had been able to put together in two hours' rush about London. Kenworthy had assembled a skeleton biography of a Parliamentary Secretary, and had sketched in some not very flattering background with the help of a political journalist.

"There's been a murder," the Commander had said.

"You surprise me. What are people coming to?"

"A tricky one, Simon. Oh, I don't think you'll have much

trouble bringing him to book. It'll probably have been done before you get there. But the county boys are anxious to side-step trouble on a national scale. That's why I want you to leave all this . . ." he indicated the desk littered with poison registers and London Underground stationmen's duty rosters, ". . . and get up there. It shouldn't take you long. According to the last census there were less than fifty inhabitants in the whole place, so that narrows it down for a start. But play it cool with Calverley. He's out to make trouble. And he's been getting himself in the news, anyway, if you can call it news."

There was a newspaper cutting from a national daily— the merest paragraph, a space-filler from a syndicated gossip column. It contained a trivial political leak; Calverley's Minister was off on a prolonged visit to the States, leaving his very junior parliamentary secretary virtually responsible for the Department and drawing attention to himself at Chequers every other weekend.

The next day, Calverley had driven north to the old man's funeral, had picked up a pair of female hitch-hikers at the roadside and treated them to an extravagant lunch in Leicester. The same journalist had reported the item, had made a song and dance about it, for Anthony Calverley's eligibility had fascinated the scandal-mongers for months. It had been assumed that he would one day, with the ice-cold efficiency that marked every step in his careerism, announce an engagement that would shoot him to the top of every tree in the forest; social, financial, even perhaps personal. But he had obstinately refused to oblige. Short of being a queer—of which there was no indication—the man seemed to want to cultivate an image of misogyny.

Kenworthy swore inaudibly at nothing and no one in particular. He disliked journalists, scandal-readers and minor politicians in about equal proportions.

But the third newspaper paragraph, after two days of journalistic silence, bore heavily on the case:

> *Few of the junior minister Anthony Calverley's most ardent admirers would claim that he is a lady's man. But many a Lothario would envy him the company of the pretty, buxom dairy-maid with whom he was seen delivering a basket of laundry in a snow-bound moorland village.*
>
> *The vital statistics were the property of his cousin, Margaret Halliwell, and the pair have been thrown together amid the shared griefs of a family funeral.*

Now Margaret Halliwell lay dead, shot at close range with a Smith and Wesson .45 of cowboy vintage, and Anthony Calverley was doing his best to make life intolerable for the county detective inspector.

Kenworthy tapped with his knuckles on the window of the car. They were now passing between close walls of snow higher than any vehicle in their convoy. Ahead of them the work was being done by a flailing mechanical plough on loan from a neighboring county council.

"A fine bloody place to go carting dirty washing about."

Wright said nothing. During the long train journey through the Midlands, and in the enforced idleness of Cotter Bridge, they had run again and again over every fact and theory that they had been able to summon out of the scanty evidence at their disposal.

With an hour or so to spare before they left St. Pancras, Kenworthy had rushed confidently to the newspaper office.

"I'll soon knock some sense out of this!"

But he had returned breathing sulphur.

"Qualified privilege! Shades of the fourth estate! . . . I

hadn't the time, Shiner—I just hadn't the bloody time. Otherwise they'd have coughed . . ."

He had drawn a blank. He had come up against a stone wall of professional protection, and had been completely unable to penetrate the anonymity of the gossip-writer.

Wright stepped gingerly through the hazards.

"Well, quite by accident, sir . . ."

In the breathless hour before departure, Kenworthy had sent him to see someone who had been at a party with Calverley on the evening before his grandfather's death: a smooth-tongued back-bencher who was counted one of Calverley's friends, but who had revealed more than he had concealed.

"The Honourable Felicity Urquhart, sir. It seems that Calverley offended her, unwittingly. Petulant little bitch, apparently. Not the sort that Calverley would normally be consorting with at all—in fact, he's a notorious woman-hater. But Shaw-Williams thought he was playing her along to get a paragraph into her column in support of his own main chance. He works like that."

"Proper basket."

"So he made some improbable date with her. And Shaw-Williams thinks she's all starry-eyed about him. Then came his mother's telephone call: she wanted him to support her at the funeral. He tried to wiggle out of it, and told her his only chance to get any real work done was when Parliament was in recess. But he had to knuckle under. So he had to break his date with the Honourable Felix. Apparently she did her nut, wouldn't believe him, asked him if he thought he was the office boy, asking for a day off. Since then, it looks as if she's been gunning for him."

"You really must choose your words more carefully, Shiner. It wasn't Calverley who was gunned."

"No, sir . . ." Wright warmed enthusiastically to his

theme, ". . . but it stands out a mile that she was jealous of this milk-maid cousin. She must have followed him up there, even to know about it."

"So she pulls a bloody great Smith and Wesson out of her West-End handbag, a thing like a portable cannon, Shiner? You could be right, but it's not my idea of poetry. Let's wait till we get up there, and hope it's all been settled for us."

Then had come the blizzard of the century, a heart-cry from the county for the Yard's assistance well out of time, then all communications ruptured, all telephone lines were down, and not even a murmur came from the county inspector's car radio.

For the hundredth time the convoy came to a halt, in the dour stone village of Anselm Norton, where snow had been cleared round recognizable relics of medieval stocks, and where cartons of bread and groceries were unloaded by men whose breath hung vaporous on the frozen air.

The Chief Constable himself, in a uniform cap resplendent with silver scrambled egg, was directing the operation. He spared a moment for Kenworthy to wind down the window.

"I'm sending the plough on ahead. That way, we shan't have so many pettifogging little hold-ups. We'll sit it out here for half an hour or so. Then we might have a clear run for the rest of the way."

Their arrival in Carrion Clough was untidy and planning broke down, largely owing to the presence in the convoy of a brewer's lorry and two television teams from rival companies, one of which seemed to value nothing more than the epic relief of the Legless Volunteer. And whilst the producer was getting in everyone's way, unloading his cameras and conscripting local men to roll barrels into the forecourt of the inn, Kenworthy caught sight of a thickset man in an opulent greatcoat, striding down to the pass that the plough had opened at the lower end of the hamlet.

"Out, quick, and stop him, Shiner!"

If Calverley was anxious to leave the village, every policeman's instinct was to keep him there. And as Wright thrust his legs out of the car, a burly man leaned in at the open door, offering a massive hand to be shaken.

"Judson, county force. We've no right, on any count whatsoever, to hold him, Superintendent. But if he once gets on the other end of a telephone, there'll be more solicitors in Carrion Clough than there are natives."

"You've not sealed things off, then?"

"Not by a long chalk."

The inspector was bluff, craggy, and must have been near to retirement. Kenworthy looked down to where Wright, after some persuasion, had at least brought Calverley to a standstill. Calverley was gesticulating wildly."

"We'd better go and give a hand," Kenworthy said. "My sergeant's learning fast, but he may still think that a parliamentary secretary is something to be reckoned with."

He introduced himself to Calverley, who swung pinkly shaved jowls in his direction.

"Scotland Yard? Well, perhaps we shall get some sense in this village at last, then. And you can begin by making sure that this young man is charged. He pulled my sleeve. That's a technical assault."

"Now, take it easy, sir. I assume full responsibility. I instructed Sergeant Wright that you must not leave the village until I had had a word with you."

"In which case, you are acting completely *ultra vires*. I have a private line to the Home Secretary, you know?"

"So have I," Kenworthy said. "Shall we believe each other?"

"Hardly the time for insolence, Superintendent."

"Hardly the time for anything but co-operation, I should have thought . . . *sir*."

Calverley looked at him aggressively, uncertain about the inflection of the *sir*. Wright looked from one to the other, slightly breathless, for he had had to run, and had headed off Calverley only by blocking with his own body the gap between a lorry and a snowdrift.

Calverley's attitude was quite different from the image Wright had conceived of the politician. Frigid self-control, ruthless careerism, were the hall-marks stressed by everyone who had made a comment. Calverley had emerged from a provincial grammar school of no reputation whatsoever to a starred first at Cambridge. In the army he had risen from conscript to brigade major, a role in which it was said that his brigadier had relied on him for a good deal more than staff work. Then he had returned to the university as a don, carrying out a *tour de force* as admissions tutor at a time when entrance procedures were being revolutionized. Nevertheless, he had found time to produce three major treatises on political economy and monetary theory. And then, suddenly, he had thrown aside the academic life: some said it was because he had spotted an obstacle to his succession to the mastership of his college. He had won a marginal seat by an improbable majority. Frigid self-control.

But Calverley's turkey-cock cheeks and blazing eyes were nearer at this moment to hysteria. Events were in control of him.

"If it comes to co-operation . . ." Calverley looked venomously in Judson's direction.

"Well, let me put it in another way, sir." There was no suspicion of innuendo this time. "I'm not likely to make any progress until I've asked you a few questions, now, am I? I can't think of anyone more likely to give me a balanced picture of what's been going on here."

Calverley's lips tightened as they might have done in accompaniment to a shoulder-shrug.

"Let's get on with it, then."

"Out here?"

The cold was bitter. Powdery snow was being whipped about their ankles.

"Let me show you your room," Judson said. "In the pub. I've had it till now, but I'm hoping to get back to HQ, just for tonight—if you can spare me, of course."

Calverley accompanied them to the inn. Isaac Pennington was posing in the doorway, and a cameraman was measuring the distance from his nose to the lens with a steel tape-measure.

"Well, now, let's get it over," Calverley said, as soon as they were in the deserted bar. "Much as I know you would like to be seeing to your own creature comforts first."

To Wright's surprise, Kenworthy did not rise to the occasion. He simply looked at Calverley in expectant silence.

"There's a half-wit in the village by the name of Booth. He's been an odd-job man about my grandfather's farm. He has unrestricted access. And he's your man. And why some people can't see it . . ."

He glowered at Judson. The inspector was unmoved.

"You're sure of this?" Kenworthy asked quietly.

"He's been spending money like water in here ever since. Old pound notes. Some of them signed by cashiers whose names haven't been seen since the nineteen-twenties. And my grandfather had a horde of these in an old metal chest in his bedroom, which hasn't been seen since the night he died. And that box also contained the Smith and Wesson."

Kenworthy looked at Judson, who showed no reaction.

"Well, I'm sure that if the inspector were even half

convinced of Booth's guilt, he'd have done something about it by now."

Judson did not speak.

"That would make the case too simple to enhance his reputation," Calverley said.

"Well, I'll go into it. If it will make you easier, I'll concentrate on Booth before I do anything else."

Calverley made a noise in his throat.

"Is there anything else?" Kenworthy asked.

"Many things." Calverley looked again at Judson. "But I shall be dealing with them through other channels."

"Well, in that case, I've neither reason nor wish to detain you."

Kenworthy's manner was so disarming that Calverley appeared not to believe him. He made no move to go.

"Of course, you are free to make whatever movements you like. If it's a phone you want, I'm afraid that you won't find one nearer than Cotter Bridge. That's seventeen miles away, but I dare say you'll have no difficulty in getting a lift, with all this transport about. And even if you can't get back tonight, there's a hotel in Cotter Bridge that I can personally recommend, provided you stay off the horseradish. I shan't be needing your help. I'll just want to put a few routine questions to your relatives."

There was not a flicker of a smile in Kenworthy's eyes, but Wright knew that the superintendent had won the round. Calverley broke out into a flurry of wrath about police ineptitude. Kenworthy quietly produced from his wallet the first of the newspaper cuttings.

"You'll have seen this, of course?"

Calverley snatched it, glanced at it, dropped it on a table.

"Utterly irrelevant."

"And this?"

Kenworthy showed him the report of his lunch party at Leicester.

"An exercise in bad taste. Which you doubtless admire."

"And this?"

Calverley had not seen the paragraphs about the milk-maid. It had been published after Carrion Clough had been isolated.

"This is absolutely outrageous. The Press Council will tear them to shreds."

"Where is she?" Kenworthy said, scarcely above a whisper.

"Where's who?"

"The Honourable Felix."

"How the hell should *I* know?"

"She must have been here. Mustn't she?"

"Impossible."

"Then how could she know?"

Kenworthy caught sight of Judson's face, and realized that the inspector was also, obviously, behind with the facts. Kenworthy passed him the cutting. The inspector's eyes clouded.

"She's not been here. No stranger *could* have been in the village without our knowledge."

"Then?"

"Someone must have phoned the newspaper."

"Someone pretty knowledgeable about what newspapers want. Anyone in the village that that fits?"

"No. I'm sure of it. The schoolmaster is the only one who's reasonably literate, and this is not his line of country at all."

Kenworthy looked quizzically at Calverley.

"Your opinion, sir?"

"I'd say the same."

"Not this man, Booth?"

"He's the village idiot! And I don't see how this by-plot can possibly help."

"The news item has some slight basis in fact, I take it?"

"I helped my cousin to carry a linen-basket. That's all."

"And were seen by?"

Calverley was obviously perplexed.

"Any villagers who might have been about in a heavy snowstorm."

"Yet it got into the London press. In next to no time. From Carrion Clough. Nothing curious about that, Mr. Calverley?"

"I see you've inquiries you must make, Superintendent."

"And I propose to look after my minimal creature comforts first."

Calverley was dismissed. He departed tamely.

KENWORTHY'S BEDROOM DESERVED preservation in a museum of social history. The bed had brass knobs and the irregularities of the mattress were apparent even beneath the contours of the eiderdown and faded patch-work coverlet. On the wall were two monochrome prints of Victorian morality: a young soldier departing for the wars from a honeysuckled cottage, with waving parents and a cherubic sweetheart. The second picture showed the warrior's return, with a moustache and a chestful of medals, the old folks not a day older, and the betrothed in the same frock.

Martha Pennington danced fussy attendance. Ten minutes after showing her guests their quarters, she was calling them downstairs to a high tea of thick slices of York ham and three fried eggs each.

"You're confident about eliminating this man Booth?" Kenworthy asked Judson.

"At the crucial moment he was in a hen-house with a hurricane lamp—gloating over the contents of the metal chest he'd stolen."

"Full of good stuff?"

"Junk. Old bills, rating assessments, receipts going back to the last century."

"Money?"

"There couldn't possibly have been any in the chest. No room. Just rubbish."

"Big disappointment for him."

"Not at all. He was bomb happy. He's simple: lives three-quarters of the time in the past. Not his own past, either. He seems in some way obsessed by the old days, older days than his. He thinks that all these papers are the title-deeds to the gathering grounds, and the old man had bequeathed them to him."

"You're certain about the timing?"

"Positive. At the time the shot was fired, Booth was half a mile away, actually being apprehended by the village bobby, whom you'll meet in due course. This metal box has been looming pretty large at the farm—as you'll gather when you talk to Edith Calverley. She'd openly accused her niece of spiriting it away."

Kenworthy stroked an egg with the prongs of his fork, and watched the golden yolk well out over the ham.

"Fill me in," he said. "Broad basis. No details at this stage. I'll read the statements later. Who did it?"

Judson pouted.

"Edith Calverley? Calverley himself? Can't have been an outsider. There aren't any outsiders."

"What sort of motive?"

"Calverley fell for his cousin. There's no doubt of that. It comes out in his every reaction. And his mother hated the girl like poison, had done for years. She takes no pains to hide it, even now the lass is dead. And her attitude to her son is possessive to the point of ridicule. She couldn't have tolerated a liaison between them. They're saying that here in the village, too."

"And Calverley?"

"*Crime* sort of *passionel*? He may have gone too far with her, then filled himself with revulsion? He's an odd man."

"Tell me about the crime."

Judson shifted his huge frame in his creaking chair.

"It was in the late afternoon, just getting dark. They'd had some sort of family row. I don't know what about. They're bloody cagey about it: say it was about this damned box, but I don't think that's true. Calverley's mother riled the girl, and she left the house in a huff. In blinding snow. Without a coat. Five minutes later—bang! They found her and the gun on a hummock just outside the farmyard."

"Not suicide?"

"Gun too far from body."

"Who found her?"

"Calverley. He and his uncle went out when they heard the shot."

"So his alibi depends on family support?"

"They'll stick together," Judson said, "even though they're the queerest mixture of folk that ever got under one roof. They're hiding something. I can feel it in my bones. . . . Superintendent, I'm glad you're here. There's something about this case that's had me doubting my own sanity. There's something crackers about the whole bloody village."

"Can you just sketch in the personalities? I'm not clear on the family relationships."

Judson wiped his plate with a hunk of bread.

"Let's start with the old man. Thomas John Halliwell. Always known by both Christian names. Mean. Tyrannical. Used to play irresponsible jokes in his younger days. They'll tell you bags of tales in there," he nodded towards the door to the public bar, "including a yarn that he'd always said they'd never bury him. That looks like becoming a legend, because up to now, it's true. They couldn't get the hearse here through the snow. So he's lying on a stone slab in what they call the dairy. Alongside his grand-daughter. At least, they're well refrigerated."

"Need a post mortem," Kenworthy murmured.

"Thought of," Judson said. "M.O. was going to follow you lot up. But whether a .45 at ten yards has left enough of her guts to see whether she was *virgo non intacta* or not, I wouldn't care to speculate."

"The old man's son's daughter?"

"That's right. Her father died in the twenties. Gassed in the first war. Her mother not long after. So she was brought up by the grandparents. Grandma died in 1942. By then she was fending for herself. Ended up by running the farm and nursing the old man almost single-handed."

"Big job."

"Yes. And by all accounts a grand lass. But when I say *farm*, don't get the wrong idea. Few hens. Three or four milk cows. Few acres of scraggy hillside, inch or two of soil. Pig or two, some years. Half a dozen ducks. No living in it. But the old man didn't need to work for a living. Only pretended he was poor. Managed to look it, too. And kept his family down to their uppers."

"How many children had he?"

"Three. Margaret's father was the eldest. Then there were two sisters. Edith was the youngest, but she's the domineering one, all the same. Prim, toffee-nosed. Holds herself all twisted up like a rifleman's pull-through. She married a man who's some sort of second-line public accountant in a Yorkshire town. He must have been quite a find for Thomas John Halliwell's girl—but, poor bastard, what he must have gone through."

"And that's the stock that's given us our future cabinet minister?"

"Future *prime* minister, *she* says."

Judson raised a pint mug of tea to his lips.

"Does Calverley dote on her?"

"There's been bad blood between them over the affair with Margaret. It's difficult to be certain just how bad. My impression is that she tyrannized him when he was a boy. And I think that since he made his own way in the world, he's kept away from home as much as he could. But she can still dictate to him. When it comes to the crunch, what she says goes. For example, when he first drove into Carrion Clough, he took a room here—your room. But she made him clear his things out and sleep up at the farm, even though that's made things pretty tight up there."

"There's another sister, too, you say? Is she at the farm too?"

"Yes. Emily. And her husband Bernard. A real London yobbo. And she's just about the opposite to Edith in every way. You'll see. I won't spoil it for you. I don't think she matters much in this case. Except, at the moment, she's as tight-lipped about the family secrets as the rest of them."

Kenworthy pushed his chair away from the table and belched gently and deliberately. He grinned mischievously at Wright.

"Well, Sergeant, what do we do now?"

There were times when he treated Wright as a benevolent medieval master might have treated an apprentice. It was a relationship that Wright was content to accept.

"Up to the farm, I should think," he said, knowing that this was the wrong answer that Kenworthy wanted him to give.

Kenworthy smiled with satisfaction.

"Let them sit up late and wonder when we're coming," he said. "I shan't go near them tonight. Bit of long-term suspense won't do them any harm, and it's the only thing that will break their silence."

He nodded to the door which led from the private quarters of the inn into the bar.

"What time does life warm up in there?"

Judson made a grunt of contempt.

"Normally there's a clientele of about six gathered by nine o'clock. Sometimes as many as eight, if it's a gala occasion. Of course, these last few nights, with the beer having run out . . ."

"Leave me your files. I'll run through them while we're waiting for the season to open."

Judson stood up.

"I'll go and see if the pathologist's arrived, and get him organized. Then I'll nip back to HQ, if I may. There's another deep frost forecast for tonight, and the roads will be impassable in another hour or so."

He opened the door, and the two Londoners looked for a few moments out into a night bleak with intense blacks and whites. Snow was beginning to fall again, delicate, gentle and persistent. On the forecourt, the drifts had been churned up by the wheels of many vehicles, and the terrain looked like the aftermath of a tank battle.

"For God's sake shut it!"

Spearheads of intolerable cold were stabbing in the draught.

"Well, how would you like Judson's life?" Kenworthy asked.

"I think he's probably a bloody good detective," Wright said, going to the root of the question.

"Yes. Orderly mind. Unexcitable. Too long in the tooth to be ambitious. What's more, he understands these people. You and I don't stand much chance, but by God, we've got to try."

He began to read the sheaf of notes and statements that Judson had handed him, grunting uninformatively at intervals, and passing each sheet to Wright as he finished it.

• 4 •

"HIS FATHER BEFORE him was a rum old bugger. Fought in the Crimea. I've heard the old folks talk about him. Didn't have much room for Thomas John."

"I've heard them say. 'One-too-many' they used to call him, when he was a lad. Wasn't wanted, see?"

In the Legless Volunteer, Haines the grocer and Ben Drabble the waterman were halfway through their first pint of the evening, telling each other stories that they both knew.

"Then Thomas John joined the army himself."

"Aye."

"That was in the South African war."

"Aye."

"Against the Boers. The old man had had the lad up on the moors, dry-stone walling. Right old slave-driver, the old man was. But they broke for bread and cheese at midday, and the old man laid himself down for forty winks, while Thomas John went out to look at some traps he'd set. And he saw a bloody great rabbit sitting up on its hind legs, chewing a weed. So he picked up a stone and threw it——"

"Bloody good shot, Thomas John was. They used to bar him from all the coconut shies and Aunt Sallies——"

"Only this time, he missed the bloody rabbit, see, and hit the old man, where he was lying. When he came up to him, he'd blood running out of the side of his head, and he thought he'd killed him, and he ran best part of twenty miles across the moors, and joined up at the first barracks that he came to. Course, he hadn't killed him, and he came back a colour sergeant, when the war was over."

Ben Drabble drank half his pint in one draught.

"And after that the pair of them got on like a house on fire. Seems the old man took a fresh fancy to the lad when he heard how he'd done as a soldier. It was about then that they started all that jiggery-pokery about the gathering grounds. Cleared up a bloody packet, the pair of them did—and ruined practically every farmer and shepherd in the Clough."

"Aye. My father always used to say no good would ever come of it. And it hasn't, has it? Thomas John never dared spend a penny."

"And they haven't buried him yet," Ben Drabble said solemnly.

"Do you think they will, then?" Kenworthy asked.

The two men turned, startled at the new voice. It was impossible to know how long the two London detectives had been in the room with them.

"It's just a manner of speaking," Haines said, in some confusion.

Wright waited expectantly. Only ten minutes previously, Kenworthy had told him that they would stand or fall by the impact of the first sentence they spoke in the bar.

"Oh, I don't know," Kenworthy said. "There are more things in heaven and earth than are dreamed of in the Criminal Record Office."

"There are that!" Drabble said, smacking his lips with emphasis.

Kenworthy looked over his shoulder at Wright, and bought drinks for the pair of them. He did not offer anything to the two local men.

"I mean," Kenworthy said, "you get pretty hard-boiled in our job. You have to be."

"Yes, I suppose you got to be."

"But you've also got to keep your mind open to lots of other things. Things that don't make any sense at all, when they first crop up . . ."

Kenworthy embarked upon a vivid and gory story about a series of cut-throat murders in a London park. Wright did not remember the case, and wondered whether the superintendent was improvising. Certainly he dwelt almost comically on some of the more revolting details. The two men listened avidly. And then Kenworthy embarked upon a pseudo-psychiatric explanation that delved three or four generations into the criminal's background.

"So, I mean to say, when Thomas John chucked a stone at that rabbit, you might say, in a manner of speaking, he killed young Margaret with it. Even though it was thirty years before she was born."

Drabble was shattered. The argument was close to his habit of mind, but remote from anything he could have thought of for himself. He could find nothing to say.

"Cause and effect," Kenworthy said, "the staff of life to any policeman. You were talking just now about some jiggery-pokery over the gathering grounds. I couldn't help overhearing you."

Wright was sure that his chief's manoeuvre had failed. In the final reckoning, any interrogation must be a brutal assault. And this one had reached that stage. Both the men were too embarrassed to answer.

"Jiggery-pokery," Kenworthy persisted. "How *could* there be any jiggery-pokery over the gathering grounds?"

"It's just what people say," Haines said, after a pause. "It's nothing to do with us. People talk. We ought to keep our big mouths shut."

Kenworthy turned his head, and looked fixedly at Ben Drabble.

"Don't ask me," Ben said. "I wasn't even on this earth in them days."

Kenworthy remained silent for long enough for the pair to be aware that he was displeased with them. Then he suddenly started reminiscing again: a story Wright knew was utterly untrue about a strangling in Bethnal Green that had had its inspiration in a drunken slander. Haines and Drabble were beginning to unwind and chuckle when the outside door opened and Wilfred Wilson ushered Tommy Booth into the bar.

Snow was caked down the front of Wilson's greatcoat and he lifted a wedge of it from the crown of his Homburg and threw it out of the door. Then he stooped to stick the poker in the fire and turned to grin at the others, treating Kenworthy and Wright as regular members of the community.

"A man must be fond of his bloody ale to turn out for it on a night like this."

Tommy Booth was merely wet and cold—he had been sheltering in the porch—and the inadequate collar of his jacket was turned up ludicrously about his neck. Tonight he went straight up to the bar and set down a coin. Isaac Pennington looked at it in amazement, then picked it up between thumb and forefinger so that the other drinkers could see it.

"Where did you get this, Tommy?"

It was a golden sovereign.

"Wages," Tommy said simply.

Pennington looked at Kenworthy for guidance, and received none. Wilson hung up his coat and came over to examine the coin.

"Probably worth about three quid, that, Tommy. What they call a collector's piece. Can't go spending it in here."

Tommy snarled, suspecting that authority was ganging up to frustrate him.

"Tell you what, Tommy, I'll give you three quid for it here and now, and I'll take it to a man I know and settle with you afterwards."

He winked openly at Kenworthy.

"Who paid you these wages, Tommy?"

"Miss Margaret."

"Not like old Thomas John's yellow box, was it?"

"No."

Tommy was truculent.

"Got to go down to Cotter Bridge about that, haven't you, Tommy?"

Tommy nodded.

"In front of the magistrates?"

"Yes."

It was simply something else that had happened to him.

"Have you got any more golden sovereigns like this?"

"Twenty, she gave me. She gave me twenty."

"Well, good luck to you!"

Wilson laughed suddenly and threw himself into a change of mood.

"Wasting bloody good drinking time in talk! What's everybody having?"

He included Kenworthy and Wright in the round, and, to Wright's surprise, Kenworthy accepted.

"Still snowing, then?" Haines asked.

"Won't be all that much. Wind's backing."

Kenworthy pulled at his pint like a man at the beginning of a solid session.

"Winters always like this up here?" he asked.

"Pretty bad. But this is quite exceptional. Worst I've known. Worse than 1935, I'd think."

Ben Drabble grunted agreement.

"There's ice down the outfall eight foot thick. I've been hammering at it all day, else they'll get no water."

Wilson stooped to remove his bicycle clips, came up panting.

"Yes. It's as if the elements had combined to give Thomas John a proper send-off. End of an epoch, that's what it is."

Tommy Booth came up already with an empty pot, slapped another sovereign on the counter. Isaac Pennington shrugged his shoulders, put the coin on a corner of a shelf away from the till and drew more beer. Tommy indicated that he wanted to buy for the others as well. Kenworthy asked for half a pint, and Wright followed his example. Wilson drained his glass gluttonously.

"I wouldn't like you gentlemen to think I usually drink at this place. But with Tommy in the chair, there's the beginning of a chance to recoup former losses."

They drank for an hour. Wright watched Kenworthy dispose of four pints and pass his glass up for more. The conversation took no useful turns, and Kenworthy made no apparent effort to guide it. And it was clear that despite his ebullience, Wilson was to a considerable extent inhibited by the presence of the Yard men.

At twenty past ten they were joined by the constable.

"Hullo, Jim. Boggarts abed?"

The policeman was distinctly embarrassed to find himself in the company of such colleagues. Kenworthy made no move to put him at his ease, and it was left to Wilson to relieve the situation.

"Come on, Jim, take that bloody silly helmet off and wrap yourself round a noggin."

After that there was a silence that Wilson could only fill with remarks of an increasingly sillier nature. Suddenly the door was flung wide open, the bar was shafted by cruelly icy air and Calverley ushered in a dapper little man in a herring-bone overcoat.

"Could I have a word with you, Superintendent?"

Calverley looked contemptuously at the half circle of empty glasses with which Kenworthy was surrounded.

"Of course."

"In private."

Kenworthy moved over and opened the door of the room in which they had eaten their high tea.

"This time, Superintendent, I'm making a protest that is going to stick. For one thing, I don't recognize an outside dairy as a proper place in which to carry out an autopsy."

The little man held out his hand.

"Dr. Carter Lyte. Consultant pathologist to M. Division. I have worked in more convenient mortuaries in my time."

"Nor do I recognize the necessity for a post mortem in a case like this. The bullet went clean through the aorta. Anyone could see that. And came out beside her spine with a hole you could get your fist in."

"I'll let you have my report as soon as it's typed," the pathologist said. "In the meantime, you may care to see this."

He brought a notebook from his overcoat pocket and handed Kenworthy an opened page. Kenworthy read it and looked coldly at Calverley.

"Have you shown him this?" he asked the doctor.

"Of course not."

Kenworthy passed it to Calverley. Calverley paled and tightened his jaw muscles.

"It'll come out at the inquest," Kenworthy said. "Perhaps at the trial, too."

Calverley said nothing.

"At least, you've enough honour—or sentiment—not to pretend it wasn't you."

There was a sudden burst of belly-laughter from the bar.

"When are you going to get down to some work, Kenworthy?"

"I'm in the middle of some at the moment."

Kenworthy edged back into the bar. The men were still laughing.

"Here's to Porcelain Palace!"

"A short, Doctor? You've earned it. Where are you spending the night?"

"Judson put me up at one of the cottages."

Kenworthy ignored Calverley. And Calverley neither wanted to stay or leave. Suddenly Tommy Booth stood up, horribly drunk.

"What was that word you said, Mr. Wilson?"

"What word?"

"That word. The end of a something, you said."

Wilson could not remember.

"End of an epoch," Kenworthy prompted.

Tommy belched.

"Epoch."

Wilson put his hand gently on the imbecile's shoulder.

"Shouldn't worry your head too much about epochs, if I were you, Tommy. What was it the poet said? 'Shoulder the sky, my lad, and drink your ale.' Well, you've had your share of wallop for one day. Now it's the sky's turn. And from what there is up there, you'll need pretty broad shoulders."

◆ 5 ◆

WRIGHT AWOKE IN a bedroom that was both very cold and very dark. The beer of the previous night had left his digestive organs utterly nauseated and the veins in his head were thumping agonizingly. It was a long and cruel orientation, drawing himself back to frozen reality from unnaturally hammered sleep.

He wondered how Kenworthy was feeling. The superintendent had put down pint after pint of mediocre ale without appearing to turn a hair. Wright groped for his electric torch and looked at his watch: six fifteen, and a day ahead of them that promised to demand every last reserve of patience and energy. He had worked with Kenworthy often enough now to know that it was courting frustration to try to make any sort of plan. One had to amble along behind like a kind of sheepdog, and yet at the same time try to anticipate and be able to fly into sudden, half-briefed action. One had to be a combination of sleeping partner and mind-reader. And the relationship was complicated further by Kenworthy's love of being exasperating out of some semi-cynical yet never unkindly sense of mischief. In this case, so far, they had done nothing. If they were near enough to Scotland Yard for the Commander to see their log, the walls and ceiling of the office would fly apart. They had not been to the scene of the crime. They had questioned none of the principals. They had measured nothing, timed nothing, written down nothing. Even the most suspicious item in the whole evidence, the apparently inexplicable newspaper cuttings, had not been followed up.

At half past seven, Martha Pennington brought him hot shaving water: a happy thought, for there was a thin layer of ice in the ewer on the wash-hand stand. He towelled himself briskly and went out on to the landing. Kenworthy's bedroom door was standing open.

"He's gone for a walk," the landlady called upstairs.

"Gone for a walk?"

"He said he wanted to see the reservoir. Breakfast is at eight."

The labyrinthine wheel-ruts on the forecourt had been frozen solid, but there had been, in fact, comparatively little snow overnight. The sky was clear now. The cold was scarcely credible.

Wright followed Kenworthy's footsteps down the lane and found the superintendent leaning on the wall, looking over the ice at the broad white sweep of the hills. Kenworthy, wrapped in a home-knitted muffler, turned his head as if he had been expecting Wright to join him.

"Cracks about brass monkeys will not be appreciated."

He waved his hand towards the panorama.

"Bloody marvellous, isn't it? I suppose. You look bloody rough, Shiner."

"I feel bloody rough."

Kenworthy laughed. Himself he was the picture of health, red-cheeked and athletic-looking, despite the fact that he was within three or four years of retirement.

"Suppose we've got to do some work today, Shiner. Otherwise we'll have Calverley after us."

Wright did not comment.

"Incidentally, I expect he'll try to get down to Cotter Bridge this morning. I'm not going to stop him, this time. He won't go far. Too scared of what we might dig out of his family in his absence."

"Up to the farm after breakfast, then?"

"Sooner or later. I want an hour or two with that school-master first."

They breakfasted on porridge, bacon and eggs and pints of tea. Wright ate slowly at first, picking up and forcing the food past his nausea to avoid Kenworthy's scorn. Then they walked the length of the hamlet towards the little school. Someone had been ridding snow from the path between the master's house and the school itself, but the job had been left half done, for a shovel and a stiff-bristled broom lay apart and askew in a drift. The door of the school stood slightly ajar, and Kenworthy led the way in.

Wilson was sitting at his magisterial desk in the single schoolroom, its walls pinned with children's Christmassy conceptions in harsh poster paint. There was a pervading smell of ink, old wood, india-rubbers and plasticine. And Wilson, palefaced, was leaning forward on his elbows, puffing out his cheeks, as if exertion had been too much for him.

"Are you all right?" Kenworthy asked.

"Aye. Yes. I'm all right. *Anno domini,* too much booze last night, and this . . ."

Wilson slid forward a letter which lay on his desk. It was a blunt statement from his education officer that a residual use for the schoolhouse had not yet been determined, but that the committee would be unable to allow him to continue to live in it after the closure of the school.

"Look, see,—*Dear Sir,*—and he's written *Wilfred* over the *Sir* in his own hand. And changed the *faithfully* to *sincerely*. Nice of him, don't you think?"

"Sad news for you. Maybe you can appeal."

"Appeal? Hell! I'm going on my hands and knees to no one."

Wilson looked pathetically round the room.

"One more lot of tadpoles—that's the only thought that keeps coming into my silly bloody head—one more lot of tadpoles. Catch the spawn at the end of March, watch their tails go and the legs come, and some of the nasty little buggers eat each other. Then set them free in the brook the day before the summer holidays. Same as every year for forty years. Only this time's the last. Don't suppose I shall be able to bring myself to keep tadpoles after I've retired."

"End of an epoch," Kenworthy said gently.

"Aye. End of an epoch. But what can I do for you, gentlemen?"

"I'm here about a murder," Kenworthy said.

"One of the foulest on the record. Or perhaps you've seen too many."

"I've seen too many. But I've never seen one that wasn't pointless. This one . . . well . . . you must have known Margaret Halliwell pretty well."

"Knew her well? Taught her in this room for nine years. My little chocolate box, I used to call her. She always had a beautifully ironed bow in her hair. Usually a blue one. Intelligent, too. There's brains in that family. It's come out in Anthony Calverley. Thomas John let his run to seed. And Margaret never stood much chance."

"She must have been devoted to the old man?"

"Devoted? Obstinately determined to do what she conceived to be her duty. Wild as the moorland wind and tough as the heather. Only a week before he died, I met her in Dick

Haines's shop. 'I'll do what I've got to, Mr. Wilson,' she said. 'But I'll not let him kill me. I've always sworn that.'"

"And who'd kill *her*?"

Wilfred Wilson spread out his hands in pathos.

"How do you volunteer to be a hangman?"

"Anybody sweet on her?" Kenworthy asked.

"Jim Russell, the village bobby, was very fond of her. We used to pull his leg about it. But he never took her out, or anything."

"Did she reciprocate?"

"She liked him, I think. I doubt whether she was greatly interested, though."

"Speaking of the village bobby, how much did you make on Porcelain Palace?"

"Don't miss any tricks, do you?" Wilson said.

"I had a couple of bob each way myself. Hundred to eight, wasn't it?"

"Paid up the night the brewer's van came to the relief of Carrion Clough. You're not going to make things tough for Russell over that, are you?"

"Mind if I smoke?" Kenworthy asked, and brought out his pipe. "Coppers on this sort of beat are not my affair. But I just wonder—Calverley and his cousin fell for each other in a big way, I believe."

"It's not my wish to pass on hearsay."

"It's more than hearsay."

"Well, if you must know. It took me by surprise. It was Tommy Booth who first told me. Said he'd seen them making merry in an old barn, behind a rusty old dray. I played hell with him. You've seen Tommy. You know what a dangerous tongue he might have. Then I heard . . ."

Wilson checked himself.

"Yes? This is a case of murder, Mr. Wilson."

"I heard they'd spent a night in his car together."

"In his car? In this bloody weather?"

"They'd had a tiff. She was taking a basket of washing up to the hall, in the snow. He followed her in that damned great car. Stopped by her half a dozen times, persuading her to get in. In the end, she did."

"What hall?"

"Warburton. About six miles, up on the moors. Commander Brayshaw. Crazy journey for him to try to make, with the weather blowing up the way it was."

"Crazier still for her to have walked, I should have thought."

"That's how they make them in these parts. If she had, she'd probably have made it. As it is, he got the car bogged down, late in the afternoon. The pair didn't show up till midday the next day."

Wright wondered whether Kenworthy would want a written statement. Judson had elicited that the car had been driven into a drift on this expedition—it had not come out that the pair had spent the night in it. But Kenworthy did not even pause to try to find out the source of information.

"Did P.C. Russell know about this?" he asked.

"I really couldn't say. Now, come, you don't think——?"

"Was Tommy Booth jealous?" Kenworthy countered.

"Tommy's in the clear, I'm told."

"On an alibi conveniently provided for him by P.C. Russell," Kenworthy said. Again, as in previous cases, Wright was staggered by the eye for salient detail.

"I wouldn't like to speculate in any of these directions," Wilson said.

"No. I wouldn't like you to, either. But I'm paid to walk all the way round everything. Incidentally——"

"You know I won't say a word, Superintendent."

"I'm sure. Calverley's been acting a bit out of character, don't you think? I hardly think of him as a philanderer."

"I'm certain he wasn't philandering with his cousin. I think he'd got it good and proper——"

"That's my impression."

"And it struck me as odd," Wilson said, "because it threw my mind back to the last time I'd seen him—the last summer holiday before the war, when he was on the verge of going to Cambridge, and came to stay at the farm and swot. Margaret was just blossoming out. A real beauty— even if her calves *were* caked with cow-muck. And young Anthony could scarcely bring himself to look at her. She told me at the time, he hardly said a word to her."

"Too conceited?"

"No. It wasn't that. He *was* conceited. But maybe he had reason to be. No. This wasn't conceit. This was just the sheer embarrassment of adolescence. His mother had sheltered him too much, for one thing. This was sex beyond his power, if you ask me. I thought so at the time. Can't I ask you in the house for a coffee?"

"No, thanks. We've got other calls to make. There's just another line of thought I'd like to clear up, though. I was talking to Ben Drabble last night."

Wilson smiled. "I sometimes think Ben believes in fairies."

"He believes something that may be right—that the roots of this murder might lie as far back as Balaclava. There must be quite a few families who had it in for the Halliwells."

"Not to the extent of murdering Margaret."

Kenworthy brought out a smoker's knife and eased the solid wedge in the bowl of his pipe.

"When I was a young detective, I used to think as you do. It didn't take me long to learn that where murder's concerned, you don't make any assumptions at all—especially honourable assumptions."

"All the same . . ."

"All the same, people have long memories—and there are some who must think that the Halliwell millions belong to them."

"The Halliwell hundreds. I don't think Thomas John ever reinvested his money into current values."

"Probably not. But that may not be generally known. The locals think that Thomas John was worth a tidy penny."

"I've heard it said."

"Well, how many of the locals come from embittered families who were dispossessed by the Halliwell machinations up on the gathering grounds?"

"I can't possibly think that——"

"Ben Drabble?"

"Ben's grandfather used to own the biggest sheep farm to the east of Black Edge. But——"

"And Dick Haines?"

"Not so affluent. But the Haineses used to farm up here. Nevertheless——"

"And yourself?"

Wilson laughed genuinely.

"Me? I'm not a native. I've only lived here forty years."

"What exactly was the nature of this Halliwell swindle?"

Wilson stood up and walked without purpose towards an unoccupied vivarium on a table by a diamond-paned window.

"I don't speak from personal experience. I'm only sixty-three."

"But you were endowed at birth with a pair of ears."

"The Water Board were interested in flooding the valley. They had to gain possession of every square inch of ground that drained into the Cotter Brook."

"I have gathered that."

"The Halliwells—Thomas John and his father—

managed to stay ahead of the Clough. They bought people out. They had private information. They passed on inspired hints, and they spread frightening rumours. They bought out the small-holders, at a profit, and they sold out to the Board. It's as simple as that."

"But remembered?"

"There's nothing else to do here but talk about the past."

"Is that why Thomas John was ashamed to spend his money?"

Wilfred Wilson picked up a little pile of elementary spelling books, and set them down on the corner of a desk.

"You're being too subtle, Superintendent."

"If I'm being too subtle, then jealousy is the only possible motive. And if that's the case, the result is not likely to be one that'll bring you personal pleasure. Was Jim Russell a pupil of yours?"

"Until he was eleven."

"And Tommy Booth?"

"I've done better with his thirst for ale than I ever did with his thirst for knowledge."

"Except for his knowledge of history."

Wilson put the spelling books back in their original place.

"You're too bloody shrewd for me, Superintendent."

Kenworthy stood up to go. But almost as an afterthought he brought out his wallet.

"What daily paper do you take, Mr. Wilson?"

"The *Daily Mail*."

"You may not have seen these, then?"

Wilson looked at the clippings through the lower half of his bi-focal lenses.

"I've seen the first two. They were passed round the Volunteer. The third's a stunner."

"Any theories?"

"Search me!"

Wilson's surprise disposed at once of any suspicion that he might have initiated the gossip item.

"The people up at Warburton Hall," Kenworthy said. "Commander Brayshaw—high society?"

"For these parts."

"The sort who might interest these column writers?"

"They spend some of the year in the West End."

Kenworthy moved towards the door.

"Six miles each way seems a fair walk to deliver laundry on foot, especially for a young lady with a farm to run and an invalid to nurse. Did Margaret do it regularly?"

"As often as not Sally Brayshaw used to slip down here in the car. There was a sort of friendship between her and Margaret."

✦ 6 ✦

KENWORTHY AND WRIGHT returned to the Legless Volunteer at a leisurely stroll, the trodden snow, with its covering of thin ice, crackling crisply under their footsteps.

Judson had just arrived, and was getting out of his car on the forecourt of the inn, cramping his bulky body to squeeze out from under the steering wheel.

Judson was proud of his overnight achievement.

"At least, I've got a car radio that works. And a replacement set if that goes wrong. So via County we can get on the G.P.O. net, too. Damned awkward not being able to make phone calls."

"Nice work, Inspector. There's a lot I want to set in motion from the London end."

"Been up to the farm yet?" Judson asked. His face fell when Kenworthy shook his head.

"No. But I shan't put it off much longer—not now I know what it is they're trying to hide."

Judson looked up with keen interest, but Kenworthy chose not to enlighten him.

"I hope you were right," Judson said, "to let Calverley get away."

"Get away?"

"They've actually got a bus through this morning. I passed it, coming up. Calverley was on it, on his way to Cotter Bridge."

"I thought he might."

"But——"

"Have you given any thought to the Warburton Hall angle?" Kenworthy asked.

"You mean the washing incident? And the possible leak to the press?"

"It seems a likely line. Can we get through to the Hall now?"

"It might be another week. Very remote. They have to prepare for siege conditions, any winter, up there. But we can phone."

"I'd hardly trust the phone for the sort of delicacy I want to cook up. And I want a little chat, as soon as we can make it, with your P.C. Russell."

"That's no difficulty. A damned good copper . . ."

"Pity. Because you may be wanting to have him suspended."

"What on earth for? Surely not for drinking after hours?"

Judson's face bore all the signs of a man for whom the honeymoon was over. The man from London was doing the dreaded thing. There would be no peace now until Kenworthy had gone home.

"No. Been drinking after hours myself, if the truth were told. And I hate myself for this, Inspector Judson—when I first cottoned on to it last night, nothing was further from my mind than taking any action on it. Passing betting slips . . ."

"The bloody young idiot!"

"Probably helps to make him a bloody good copper, as a matter of fact. I'm the hypocrite. But I may want him on a fizzer for it. I'll let you know, when I've had five minutes with him. You see, he's emotionally involved in this case. And that won't do. Won't do at all. Will it, Inspector? Now where can I find Tommy Booth?"

Judson gave him directions.

"Want me to come?"

"No, thanks. I may be a hard bastard, but I'm going to play it very gently with Tommy. Shan't even want Shiner with me. Now if you, Inspector, will make it top priority to get hold of Russell for me . . ."

"He'll be here within the hour."

"Put the wind up him, without giving him a clue what it's about."

Kenworthy stalked off in the direction of the Booths' cottage, leaving Wright without a chore, without an instruction, without even a pastime. It was too cold to stay out of doors without urgent cause. It was more than his life would have been worth to have made any approach to any of the characters who would have to be questioned at pressing speed within the next few hours. He went into the Legless Volunteer and Isaac Pennington was mopping out the bar. He went into the room in which they took their meals, and Martha had all the furniture topsy-turvy and the carpet up. He went up to his bedroom, and some old crone had all his sheets on the floor.

So he went back out into the cold, sauntered over to the spot where he had stood with Kenworthy earlier in the morning, bought cigarettes at Dick Haines's store, walked to the dam at the end of the reservoir, and talked to Ben Drabble, whose chest and shoulders emerged from a brick-arched culvert.

"I'll swear it's never been like this in my lifetime, or in the lifetime of this waterworks."

He brought up a solid block of ice, at least a cubic yard, and threw it out into the snow.

"It's taken me two hours to chip that out, and that's only the surface. I ought to light a fire down here, but I'm frightened for the masonry. There's ice in the fissures. God knows what will happen when the thaw does come."

"How deep is the reservoir?" Wright asked.

"Seventy feet in the middle. Shelves away very abruptly after about ten yards from the bank. And it's two miles seven furlongs from here to the next lodge. That's a hell of a head of water."

Wright walked back to the inn, hoping for some corner or other where the cleaning was complete. Isaac Pennington was still hard at work, but saw his predicament, and placed a hard wooden chair for him in a corner. Wright sat and did nothing, then got out his notebook, and for no great reason began to make a list of suspects. *Calverley: Edith Calverley; Booth; Drabble; P.C. Russell; Felicity Urquhart*. After a pause he added: *Wilfred Wilson*, then tore out the page, screwed it up and set fire to it in an ashtray.

Half an hour later, Kenworthy came in, looking decidedly pleased with himself despite a display of ferocious disgust.

"Well, let's hope we can close this case without having to put *him* in the witness-box!" He laughed uproariously. "There are some Q.C.s I'd like to see tackle him."

"He sent you up the wall, did he?"

"Oh, no. Oh, no. We came to a close understanding, Tommy and I. Blood brothers, you might say. Another ten minutes with him, and he'd have been the one who'd have been sorry for *my* mental state. Do you know what, Shiner? He really does think that the old man left him all these bloody moorlands and he thinks he's going up in front of the beaks at Cotter Bridge to get it all sorted out in his favour."

"*You* told him that, didn't you, sir?"

One had to be a supreme judge of Kenworthy's moods to know when one dared be flippant with him.

Kenworthy smiled sadly.

"Well, I had to prove somehow or other that I'm on his side."

"And are you?"

"I don't know, Shiner. I honestly don't know. This is getting too convoluted for me. I'm beginning to think I must have a left-hand thread. Just suppose, Shiner, that Russell had fixed an alibi for him, and yet didn't kill the girl himself. Does that mean that Tommy might have done it after all?"

"How can we tell, without further evidence? What would Russell want to do a complicated thing like that for?"

"To cover up some other dark and dismal carry-on."

"Such as?"

"I don't know. It's just surmise."

"You're on to something, aren't you, sir?"

"No," Kenworthy said. "Nothing that I think matters, anyway."

"Tommy Booth's given you some new idea about the case."

"About the case, Shiner, about the case? You don't think I've been crouching with Tommy Booth in a bloody henhouse talking about the case, do you?"

"You must have talked about something."

"About a shop in the village where you could buy whipcord, and glass marbles, and strings of squibs. Not in *this* village, and not a shop that Tommy's ever seen. One under the water. And if Tommy had brought one of the glass marbles out of his pocket, I'd have been ready to believe he'd just bought it. And he also saw Ben Drabble's grandfather and a man called Caleb Wardle, come out of Smithy Lane this morning, stop at the top of Barrow Brow, and point to a crack in the weathervane of the church."

"Very useful."

"Vital," Kenworthy said. "Because it was you and me he saw. The timing was exact. I checked on it. And, if you remember, I did sweep my hand up in the direction of the gathering grounds. That was Caleb, indicating the steeple."

"As you say, sir—vital."

"Seriously, though, Shiner, don't you see where we might go from here?"

"Colney Hatch."

"You don't think we might turn the case on Abraham Drabble and Caleb Wardle?"

"We might turn something."

"Just let me get my scalpel into that Jim Russell's ribs," Kenworthy said darkly, and did not speak again until Judson brought the policeman into the bar, some quarter of an hour later.

There was no doubt that the county inspector had discharged well his task of fraying Russell's nerves. The man in uniform was white-faced, his knuckles were tightly clenched, his eyes strayed to inanimate objects as if he thought he was looking at them for the last time.

"Sit down, Constable," Kenworthy said sweetly. "That's a nice chestful of ribbons you have there. S.E.A.C., obviously."

"Did a bit in Burma, sir."

"Chindit?"

Russell nodded, beginning to feel more at ease.

"So you joined the force after your demobilization?"

"That's right, sir."

"Local man?"

"Born and bred here."

Kenworthy turned to Judson.

"Isn't it a trifle unusual to employ an officer on his own manor like this?"

"Recruitment is so bad, we've had to relax a number of things, Superintendent."

"Where do you live, Constable?"

"Anselm Norton, sir."

"That's about six miles down the road, isn't it?"

"Sir."

"How often do you visit Carrion Clough?"

"Most days, sir."

"You were at school here?"

"Yes, sir."

"So you'd have known Margaret Halliwell well."

"At school together, sir."

"But she was younger than you."

"There was only one class in our school, sir."

"Have you ambitions in the force?"

"I've passed for sergeant, sir. Waiting for a vacancy."

Judson nodded confirmation.

"You might have to wait a long time," Kenworthy muttered equivocally, then suddenly snapped: "Who's your bookie?"

Russell flinched. It was scarcely perceptible—but he flinched. Judson kept his eyes fixed on him, expressionless.

"I'm sorry, sir," he said, then paused. "Well, that's all I can say, sir, isn't it? I'm sorry. I know what this is going to mean."

Kenworthy suddenly changed his tone, speaking slowly and imperatively.

"Why did you go up to Moss Farm on the night the old man died?"

Russell did not hesitate.

"To ask Margaret Halliwell for money."

"Because you knew Thomas John was dying?"

"No. It had nothing to do with Thomas John dying. When I saw her leave the house, I knew that he must have gone, and I kept out of her sight."

"You got money from her afterwards?"

"No, sir. How could I, after . . . ?"

"Did anyone see you go up to the farm?"

"Somebody must have."

"Any idea?"

"No, sir."

"Tommy Booth. Only he mistook you for a Grenadier sergeant. Because of your helmet. Just as he thought I was Abraham Drabble and Sergeant Wright was a character called Caleb Wardle. Tommy sees things that aren't there—but something has to trigger them off. See?"

"Yes, sir."

Russell breathed and exhaled deeply.

"Anything else to tell me, Constable Russell?"

"Only why I wanted the money, sir. It was that last bet. I hadn't laid it. I was standing it myself."

Judson caught his breath. Russell seemed not to notice.

"There were a lot of people on. Wilfred Wilson had a fiver, and it caught on. Hundred to eight. That was forty quid for a start. If only I could have kept them waiting a few days, but I daren't."

"The blizzard came a day or two too late for you, eh?"

Russell did not understand at first, then he said, "Yes, sir," almost mechanically.

"So what did you do for money?"

"Sold my motor-scooter, sir."

"At a loss, no doubt?"

"Didn't haggle, sir."

Kenworthy sat with his cheek cushioned in the palm of

his hand, and did not change his facial expression or speak a word for the space of ten seconds.

"Well, Constable Russell," he said at last, "the sooner we get you out of this uniform, the better. That's if it is agreeable to Inspector Judson?"

Judson assented miserably.

"I knew it had to come to this," Russell said.

"Come to what?"

"The chop."

"Who said anything about the chop? You're an honest man. A fool—but an honest man. I want you in plain clothes, as an *aide*. I suppose the Chief Constable will wear it?"

"That depends," Judson said, "on how much the Chief Constable gets to know. I can fix the plain-clothes bit on my own initiative."

"Do that, then. P.C. Russell knows well enough in what circumstances this conversation need not be remembered."

Kenworthy looked at his watch. And even as he did so, Pennington went and threw open the bolt of the main door.

"If ever a man was due for a hair of the dog!" Kenworthy said. "I'm not like Sergeant Wright, here. Up in the morning bright and early, looking as if he was on lemonade all night."

He bought them a pint of bitter each, and scarcely was the foam off the top of their glasses than Calverley came in, escorting a short but sturdy old man who was wrapped up to the ears in worsted.

Calverley looked significantly at the policemen's pots.

"Could you manage a couple of lunches, landlord, please? We'll eat in here. I've no wish to horn in on a private party."

"I think that will be all right, Mr. Anthony. I'll just ask the missus."

"What do you want me to do?" Russell asked.

"Back to duty, till you hear from us," Kenworthy said.

Wright looked covertly at Calverley's companion. He was a man of well over seventy, with a hale complexion and a mass of well kept white hair. He was wearing a stiff butterfly collar and obviously belonged to a forgotten world.

Russell finished his drink and left. The parties separated for lunch.

"I'd like to thank you for that," Judson said, over roast beef and towering Yorkshire pudding.

"For what?"

"For salvaging that young man's career. Mind you, I'm not easy about it. If there's ever a complaint . . ."

"If we do him for murder, we can ride the complaint."

"Do him for murder?"

"I don't *think* he did it," Kenworthy said. "But he's too promising a candidate to ignore. I'm going to give him a few little jobs to do that will produce some interesting reactions. Who's Calverley's pal, by the way?"

"Horncastle. The Halliwells' solicitor. From Cotter Bridge. Wouldn't take him for eighty-three, would you? Still walks three miles a day. The clerks in his office used to have to show him their old pen-nibs before he would issue them with a new one. And that went on right up to 1939."

"The reading of the will, I suppose. That's something I'm going to gate-crash, Judson."

Judson raised his eyebrows, opened his mouth, then said nothing. Wright wondered what he really thought of Kenworthy.

"You'll be needing me?"

"For an hour or so. After that, it's more important that you should get the paperwork behind Russell's transfer organized. And as soon as you do, get him to work on two pairs of snow-shoes."

"Snow-shoes?"

"Yes. You know, those things Canadian trappers wear. Look like tennis rackets. Get him to start with barrel hoops, or something. Make a network of old rope, or thongs of something or other, then tie a pair of shoes inside. Something to distribute his weight. Go to the public library, if he hasn't a clue. Something to stop him sinking up to his knees every time he puts a foot forward. He's going to take Shiner for a long, cool walk."

• 7 •

KENWORTHY ROSE FROM the meal-table with unexpected brisk-ness, put on his overcoat and scarf and led Wright and Judson through the public bar, at one of whose tables Calverley and the lawyer were taking their time over coffee.

He walked quickly across the road and headed straight for the steep lane which climbed up to the farm. It was hard walking, not only because of the gradient, but also because every few yards they had to stop and knock off huge balls of compressed snow which kept forming under the heels of their shoes. Nevertheless, Kenworthy managed to keep a stride or two ahead of his companions, Judson wheezing unashamedly, and even Wright feeling the tightness of lungs charged with intolerably icy air.

"By God," Judson said, "some people keep in training."

Kenworthy grinned.

"It takes a Londoner. You hill-folk don't get enough exercise."

They stopped by a gate to take a fresh breath, looked out over the snow-bound fells, below them the road and the roof of the Volunteer, stretching away to their left the white expanse of the reservoir. The tracks of a hare trailed across the corner of a field. They could see the depressions in the snow where he had stopped at intervals to rest his rump.

"You just can't," Kenworthy said. "You just can't make a living up here."

"A lot of hard lives," Judson said.

"Yet people stay. People were fighting tooth and nail to stay, when the Water Board were turning them off. Over fifty years ago, and there's still bitterness."

He looked at his watch.

"Don't want to rush you, but I'd like to beat those two. If Calverley knew what I had in mind, they'd be shooting up here like rockets."

They reached the gate of the farmyard, which Wright held open for the others. Tall metal milk-churns stood on a wooden platform. An old dray had been drawn from a long, open barn, in which they could see tyre-marks.

"What does he drive?"

"Austin Princess."

"You've had a look at it?"

"Can't get at it. Miles up on the moors. There are probably drifts over its roof by now."

"Russell and Wright are going to need their snow-shoes."

Blue smoke was rising idly from a chimney of the farm, hanging almost motionless over the slate roof. Snow bulged over the eaves, softened by the heat of the house.

"The bodies are in there," Judson said.

The dairy was an outhouse. The corpses were on scrubbed stone slabs that ran along either wall. A wooden hand-churn stood in a corner. The old man was already in his coffin, whose lid was standing against a whitewashed wall. The girl's body had been covered with white linen cloths below the chin.

"She was a good looker," Kenworthy said. "I can see what got into Calverley."

Then they heard the click of the gate-latch. Calverley and Horncastle came across the yard. Calverley was talking in his best professional drawl, impressing the lawyer by treating him as of his own standing.

"Of course, it's not my department, so it would be irresponsible of me to make any promises. But I can at least cut a few corners for you. I'll be in Cotter Bridge tomorrow morning, and I'll drop in and look over the papers. As I said just now, your U.D.C. can't begin to contemplate action without a private act of parliament. And I can think of half a dozen ways of putting that off for years."

"Big stuff," Judson said.

"Highly convincing. How big a man is Horncastle?"

"Worth about a quarter of a million, rumour goes."

"In Cotter Bridge? Must be an extensive practice."

"Conveyancing, mostly. But that's not where the money is, not out of his own clients. Real estate: knowing where to buy, what to corner and when to sell."

"Like the gathering grounds?"

"That was Horncastle's father. This one was just out of his articles in those days."

Kenworthy grunted. They heard the pair knock the sides of their shoes against the door-post and enter the house.

"Let them get settled. There's no point in interrupting until there's something to interrupt. Take me and show me the spot."

Judson conducted them round the corner of the dairy, obliquely past the front of the house, past a row of empty pigsties, over a stile, across the corner of a field and through a wicket-gate in a heavily burdened hedge. The snow underfoot had been well trodden, and such as had fallen since the main events had scarcely filled the concavity of earlier footprints.

They climbed a bulging knob of land, to where a gnarled old tree commanded the sky-line. There was a huge spreading pink stain where she had fallen backwards into the snow.

"This was where Calverley found her?"

"You can see, Superintendent."

"It took him how long?"

"Five to ten minutes, he said."

"In a blizzard?"

"Blinding. They are all agreed on that."

"He must have known where she was coming. There are no signs that his tracks veered either to right or left."

"That had occurred to me. If you remember, I mentioned it in my report."

"Extraordinary. I like extraordinary things. They're usually extremely helpful. That tree's hollow. . . ."

"Struck by lightning."

Kenworthy extended his arm and thrust his hand into a hole in the bark on a level with his head. He brought it out again and looked at his finger-tips in disgust.

"Owl pellets," Judson said.

"If she had anything to hide—such as the money that ought to have been in the chest or perhaps the gun itself—she might have chosen just this place. I suppose she might even have taken Calverley into her confidence, the way things went between them. Come; it's time we chucked a pebble into the mill-pond."

Kenworthy led the way back to the farmhouse and hammered on the door with the side of his fist. The noise reverberated round the sheds and barns and seemed to bring him a boyish enjoyment, for he looked round smiling mischievously and beat a second, quite unnecessary salvo.

The door was opened to them by a little man in a brown suit with a black tie and a few strands of hair brushed across his bald head.

"Mr. Bernard Pollard?" Kenworthy asked in friendly fashion, and extended his hand heartily.

They looked into a large farmhouse kitchen, stone-flagged, but well strewn with thick rugs of coloured wool-clippings. On one wall were framed crossed flags, the Union Jack and old Thomas John's regimental colours, lovingly embroidered in silk. And there was a picture illustrating the "Mistletoe Bough," with a tall, aristocratic young lady standing by an empty, open oak chest. The verses of the old ballad were printed in small type beneath it. On another wall was a Victorian illuminated version of the Lord's Prayer in an elaborate and amateurish hand-carved frame.

Heat welled towards them from a huge, black-leaded kitchen-range. Pollard nervously took a step backwards. Calverley came angrily through a door which led into a small parlour.

"Really, gentlemen, this is monstrous. You knew very well how we were going to be occupied for the next half-hour."

"I'm sorry," Kenworthy said, in his softest tones. "But this is urgent."

"Urgent? You have done nothing but drink and idle since you arrived in the village yesterday evening. Now you have the nerve to speak of urgency. . . ."

Kenworthy muttered something deliberately unintelligible, in which the words *murder* and *vital evidence* were distinctly audible. By now he had manœuvred his party across the breadth of the kitchen, and they were looking into the parlour, with its horse-hair upholstery, its American rocking-chairs and antimacassars. Edith Calverley was sitting upright and tightlipped in a shapeless dress of black satin. Beside her her sister, a spreading peroxide blonde, was looking rather frightened, and had evidently recently shed a tear or two of sentimental propriety. Opposite the women were two vacant chairs left by Pollard and Calverley, and at the head of the table sat Horncastle, looking at once benign and diabolic, with his hearty red face and his shock of white hair combed up at unusual angles.

"This is a private family occasion," Calverley said.

"This is a public inquiry."

"You have no right whatsoever . . ."

Kenworthy beamed at them amicably.

"I have not, to my knowledge, tried to assert any rights. I have merely knocked on a door, and took it that an invitation to enter was implicit—under the circumstances."

Horncastle looked up over the rims of his spectacles.

"I would suggest, Mr. Anthony, that we set chairs for these gentlemen and ask them to sit patiently by whilst we conduct our little business. It will not take five minutes. The contents of this," he indicated the will, lying on the table in front of him, "are neither secret nor sensational, and are about to become public knowledge."

Edith Calverley pressed the nails of her curled fingers into her cheek.

"Of course, they must stay, Anthony. Mr. Horncastle is right. We have nothing to hide."

Calverley's shoulders jerked. He sat down in his place again, making no move to put chairs for the detectives. Pollard began quickly to move furniture about. Kenworthy nodded to Horncastle that as far as he was concerned the proceedings could begin.

The reading of the will was an anti-climax. Wright assumed that the whole purpose of Kenworthy's tactic had been to catch the immediate reaction of individuals to any unorthodox legacies, so he, too, watched their faces intently. But there was not an item to rouse even the faintest tremor of jealousy or surprise. Thomas John Halliwell had, in the year 1926, declared himself sound in body and mind, and had bequeathed the whole of his worldly substance to his wife. In the event of her having predeceased him, his wealth was to be divided equally between the issue of his body, or their survivors. Was there the suggestion of a sigh of relief round the table? Had they expected the old man's testament to be the last of his intricate and tasteless practical jokes?

The tension was relaxed. Edith Calverley rose to bring a tray of slender glasses and a bottle of ginger-wine. Kenworthy drew his chair up to the table as if he now considered himself one of the family.

"You know, Mr. Horncastle, in my experience, men like T.J. are often loth to make wills. They don't like thinking in terms of the death-bed. It seems like tempting providence."

"That is all too often so," the solicitor said, in slow, pedantic tones.

"As often as not, it's some sort of personal crisis, something emotional, and perhaps curiously irrelevant, that brings them to the point."

"I have known that to happen."

"Well, now, January 27th, 1926. That's over thirty years ago. You drew up this will yourself?"

"That is so."

"He had had, perhaps, an illness? A winter ailment?"

Kenworthy seemed to be slipping into archaisms to match the lawyer. Horncastle smiled thinly.

"There was nothing like that. I had tried for years to make him see the wisdom——"

"And he came round suddenly, just like that?"

"Not suddenly, Mr. Kenworthy. It was at least the sixth time he had come to my office for this express intention. I had never previously succeeded in bringing him to the point." He smiled. "Simple though it all is, Mr. Kenworthy."

Kenworthy tilted his chair backwards and looked happily round the table.

"You mean, it would be simple, if you could only find the money."

Calverley rose from his sulky silence.

"If *we* can find the money? I suppose we've got to forsake hope of receiving any help."

Kenworthy stood up.

"Bit difficult. In all this snow. Well, ladies and gentlemen, I thank you."

Calverley turned on him.

"Superintendent, I cannot understand your casual attitude. Since last night we have been holding ourselves in readiness."

"In readiness?"

"Do we not assume that you wish to question us?"

Kenworthy looked from one face to another.

"Well, since you're inviting me to stay. If I might use this room? I'd like to see you one at a time. Starting with you." He turned to the frightened Pollard. "And Inspector Judson, I think now, if you've any business to attend to down in Cotter Bridge . . ."

◆ 8 ◆

"RUM BLOODY LOT you married into."

Alone with Wright and Pollard, Kenworthy forsook whimsicality. Pollard did not know what he was expected to reply.

"Londoner, aren't you?"

"Dalston," Pollard said. "East eight."

"You'll have heard of me, then."

Pollard's facial expression showed that this was indeed the case.

"Dalston: Lavender Grove, Wilton Way, Lansdowne Drive. One of the first cases I handled as a detective sergeant was in Colvestone Crescent."

The local colour did nothing to lighten Pollard's unease. He lived not a stone's throw from some of the streets whose names Kenworthy was bandying about.

"Not that I'm difficult to get on with. Ask Tom Brent in the Brickmaker's Arms. Know him? Just as long as people don't hold out on me."

There was a short silence.

"I'm not holding out on you," Pollard said.

"Of course. I know you wouldn't. How did you come to meet the Halliwells?"

"It was in the First World War. We was in camp up here, see?"

"Your wife's a different proposition from her sister," Kenworthy said.

"You can say that again."

"It remains to be seen whether you're more scared of Edith than you are of me."

He allowed Pollard to ponder the meaning of this for a few seconds, then stepped up the speed of his questioning.

"The night young Margaret was killed. Tell me what happened."

"We heard the shot, see?"

"Before that. Before she went out of the house."

Wright was studying Pollard carefully. There was just a slight twitch in his facial muscles, that might mean that he found the shift in emphasis discomforting.

"There was a row. There was always a row. Edith didn't like the girl."

"'Cause why?"

"'Cause why—I don't know. 'Cause she thought she might have pulled a fast one, living so close to the old man, and he might have left her the lot. As far as Emily and me were concerned, well, I said to Emily on the way up here——"

"And this particular row. What was it all about?"

Kenworthy and Wright both looked steadily at him. This was a Kenworthy move that Wright knew: the cornering of the unpractised liar. There is nothing the amateur loathes so much as the lie direct; anything is preferable—the half-truth, the "might have" or the self-deception of uncertainty. Pollard was a moderately honest man. The blunt question and the two pairs of eyes had him cornered. There was another pause, the momentary protrusion of the tip of his tongue over his lips.

"About the box," he said. "We've heard nothing but that blooming box since we arrived."

"What did Edith say about the box?"

"Said Margaret had pinched it."

"But she'd been saying that all along, you said. What was there so special about it this time, to drive her out into the snow?"

"I suppose she was just fed up of hearing about it."

"What were the actual words that Edith said?"

"I can't really remember."

"You could if you tried."

"Called her a tea-leaf."

"Those aren't the actual words."

Kenworthy suddenly shot his elbow onto his knee, not really an aggressive gesture, but one sufficiently suggestive for Pollard.

"She said, 'You're a dirty little thief'," he said.

"Whereupon she dashed out into the yard?"

Pollard nodded.

"Without a coat?"

"That's right."

"And no one thought of going after her?"

Pollard was worried by the question.

"Anthony wanted to," he said, "but his mother wouldn't let him."

"You're asking me to believe that a man of his age and standing, who was clearly in love with his cousin, was afraid of offending his mother at a moment like that?"

"Well, they were shouting at each other, and he kept edging to the door, had it open once but the snow kept blowing in—she kept him arguing, you see. It was only, like, for a minute or two. Then . . . ."

"You heard the shot?"

Pollard agreed, and looked away. He was more deeply involved emotionally than one might have imagined.

"Who went out?"

"Anthony and me."

"Which way did *you* go?"

"Into the dairy and the barn."

"Of your own accord? Or did Anthony send you there?"

"He told me to go there."

"And he went—made a bee-line, in fact—for the place where it happened?"

"That's right."

"As if he'd known?"

"He said, 'She'll have gone up to the tree. I'll go up to the tree.'"

"Why should he think she'd gone to the tree?"

"She was always going to the tree."

"Why?"

"I can't explain, really. It was, sort of, kids' stuff, you know."

"No, I don't. But I'll find out."

Then Kenworthy relaxed.

"Do you like this part of the world?" he asked.

Pollard reverted to type.

"Do I buggery! All I want's to get back to the bloody Smoke."

"Those are my sentiments exactly," Kenworthy said. "So let's get on with the job. Would you go and send your wife in, please?"

Pollard hesitated at the door.

"Don't be too bloody hard on her, Super."

"I wasn't hard on you, was I—in spite of the load of bloody cod's wallop you've been trying to fill me up with?"

Emily Pollard came and sat down gingerly on the edge of

one of the American rockers. The contrast between her and her sister was no less striking for a second chance to examine her. Wright wondered if perhaps she took after her mother; he had seen enough of Thomas John's corpse to know where Edith's resemblance lay.

Emily was flabby, fair-skinned and made up cheaply, though not quite garishly. Lipstick was thick and shiny about her weak mouth. Rouge was pink, in clearly demarcated patches high about her cheek-bones. She had heavy rings on the fingers of each hand, none of them worth more than a shilling or two. At very close quarters her age showed through—she must have been in her later sixties, for she was older than her sister. The tendons of her neck belied her camouflage, and the veins at the base of her fingers were blue and distended.

"I suppose I can smoke?"

She was volatile; she was nervous, but she was going to put on a blasé act. Wright saw that Kenworthy was going to play her gently.

"This must remind you of winters you knew as a girl, Mrs. Pollard."

She shuddered playfully.

"Do you often come back to Carrion Clough?"

"No, not very often."

"When was the last time?"

"Rather a long time ago, I'm afraid. This place always gives me the screaming ab-dabs."

"How long ago? Five years? Ten?"

"Let me see, now when was it?"

"Since the war?"

"I should hope so. What do you take me for? Well, it would be the first summer after the war."

"So this old house has got some rather sad associations for you?"

"Oh, well, I wasn't born here, you know. I was eight or nine when we moved here."

"So you can remember the old village?"

"Bits of it."

"Like the little shop on the corner of Smithy Lane, where you could buy whip-cord, and glass marbles and strings of squibs?"

"God!" she said, "you must have second sight."

"That's what they pay me for. And that's how I know that your naughty little husband told me one or two rather important little fibs."

"The fat-head!" she said, and then, "Oh, but Bernie wouldn't——"

"Bernie did! And I hope that you're going to show a bit more savvy. Now I want you to tell me what happened in the half-hour before Margaret was murdered."

"I knew you'd get on to that," she said, pointlessly. "There'd been a bit of a scene. It's Edith, you know. She means well, and she has a heart of gold. But she does go on a bit."

"She didn't like your niece, I gather?"

"Oh, that's putting it a bit hard. She thought she'd have brought her up a bit differently if she'd been her own. Well, I know what *I* think. But Edith's one who has to have her own way. And Margaret was always independent."

"And what was the row about this time?"

"The box. My father's old tin chest. She thought Margaret had helped herself to it."

"And became insulting about it?"

"She wasn't very nice."

"Her precise words?" Kenworthy asked, distantly yet firmly.

"She called her a thieving young bitch."

"I see. Thank you. And after that?"

"After that? Well, Margaret flew out of the house. Banged the door."

"And none of you tried to stop her?"

"It wasn't much use."

"No one thought of trying to fetch her back?"

She shook her head.

"Not even Anthony?"

"Oh, well, Tony did get up."

"And?"

"Well, he went to the door, and—Edith was in a screaming rage by now. Tony had to try to calm her down."

"What sort of things were they saying to each other?"

"On, I can't remember now."

"You'd better, Mrs. Pollard. Because if it were to enter my head that Tony had left the house *before* that shot was fired—"

"Oh, but Mr. Kenworthy, of course he didn't. We were all there together."

"But if he hadn't stopped to argue with his mother, he *would* have left the house before the shot was fired, wouldn't he? And then I should be having to ask some awkward questions, shouldn't I? So please try to remember. What did they say to each other?"

"Edith said she was only a little thief, and wasn't worth bothering about, and Tony said she was his cousin and he wasn't going to have her talked to like that."

"Sounds pretty lame to me," Kenworthy said. "However, perhaps one of the others has a better memory. All right, Mrs. Pollard. Thank you. I'll let you know if I think of anything else."

She stood up, ready to go, and then seemed unwilling to leave them.

"Yes, Mrs. Pollard?"

"Nothing."

She turned her back on them and crossed the floor to the door as if it were a long, lonely walk she was taking.

◆ 9 ◆

"That tree, Mrs. Calverley, near where poor Margaret was found. It's hollow."

"I know. That's where the gun was hidden."

"You don't surprise me. The money too, I wouldn't wonder."

"No, it wasn't. I'd looked."

Edith was frigidly, nastily honest about it. She sat in one of the less inviting chairs, looking from Kenworthy to Wright with distasteful appraisal.

"Tell me about the gun," Kenworthy said.

"It was something my father had picked up in his wanderings. He'd never used it. Of course, he'd never used it. But it was always in the chest, and sometimes he used to talk about it. It used to scare my poor mother to death, and us children. And Margaret. I'm not surprised she wanted to get it out of the house as soon as she could."

"Now tell me about the tree."

"The tree? A tree's a tree."

"A hollow tree."

"There's nothing unusual in that," she said.

"Burned out by lightning. When did that happen?"

"Before I was born."

"So you remember it, when you were a child?"

"Of course I do. What *is* all this about? We used to play round it."

"So did Margaret in her turn, I expect."

"I expect so. Yes, as a matter of fact, she did. A lot."

"Yes," Kenworthy said. "I thought that tree loomed rather large in her existence. When you're as lonely as young Margaret must have been, it's surprising what a staunch friend you can make out of a tree."

Edith looked at him unmoved, not even displaying surprise at the turn the questioning was taking. Then, as if on an afterthought, she volunteered an anecdote.

"It's strange you should say that. On the night I arrived here, the Rector called. He'd cycled at least six miles—that was before the snow—and I asked him to say a prayer. And of course, I expected Margaret to join us. But would she? Flounced out of the house, just as she did the last time. It wasn't her fault, of course, she was brought up a heathen. I had to go out and look for her, in case she should catch cold. And I found her standing by the tree, mooning, looking out across the reservoir. And nearly dark, too."

"Yes," Kenworthy said, "that explains how your son knew where to go and find her. He knew your niece better than you think, Mrs. Calverley."

This time she did preserve her silence.

"Don't you have a little twinge of conscience," Kenworthy asked, "thinking that you sent her out to her death?"

"She went of her own accord. And I don't know who killed her—but he'd have done it sooner or later, I suppose."

"Why should he? Can you offer me a theory about that?"

"For the money. What else? I don't know what carryings-on

she had when we weren't here. It must have been someone who knew her well enough to know where she'd hidden the gun."

"Indeed it must," Kenworthy said, a good deal more pointedly than she appeared to notice. "And the final quarrel that led to her rampaging out of the house?"

"I was asking her again about the box and the money. She had taken it, and she had no right to. I'm sorry for what's happened. I am horrified. I don't know when I shall ever have a full night's sleep again. But it cannot alter the plain fact——"

"What was it you called her? A whore, was it? Or a harlot?"

"I beg your pardon?"

"I'm only guessing," Kenworthy said. "It wasn't a thief, I know that."

"I don't know what you're talking about. I shall call my son . . ."

Kenworthy stood, and moved unobtrusively between her and the door.

"All to protect his political career," he said.

"I beg your pardon?"

"You and your family, Mrs. Calverley, have been indulging in a conspiracy that has cost Inspector Judson and myself several hours of work. You have invented the quarrel about the box, in order to try to conceal the fact that Anthony and Margaret spent a night together in a comfortable and roomy car. I will grant you that you probably did not think it mattered very much, that it could not affect the main issue. But I prefer to ferret things out as they were and are."

She did not reply. She did not betray whatever shock she may have felt. She simply waited for Kenworthy's next move.

"Fortunately," Kenworthy said, "not all your relatives are as reliable and tight-lipped as you might have hoped."

Again, she gave no inkling of the hell she must have been preparing for Bernard and Emily.

"But you can be grateful for one thing," Kenworthy said. "They all stick to their guns that you didn't rush out to bring Margaret back. No one remotely suggested that you might have left the house before the shot was fired. That, I fear, is going to be an uphill furrow for us to plough."

Calverley's figure appeared round the door almost before his mother had left the room. But Kenworthy had already risen, and was blowing down the stem of his empty pipe. Wright closed his notebook; it was policy, apparently, to keep Calverley on tenterhooks still.

"I hope you're not going to smoke that thing in here," Calverley said.

"Of course not. Just getting ready to pollute the fresh air with it."

"From which I gather that you're leaving."

Kenworthy looked at him with long, cold insolence.

"Have you anything to add to your previous statement, the one you made to Inspector Judson?"

"At this stage, no."

"That is what I thought."

Wright followed him through the farmhouse kitchen. Emily was smoking heavily. Pollard was pretending to be interested in a newspaper. Edith had put on a pinafore, and was preparing to make pastry on a scrubbed deal table. Kenworthy wished them a courteous, if unnecessarily hearty good day, and himself opened the door.

He did not speak until they had crossed the yard and were back among the deeper snow at the top of the steep lane.

"Well, the cat's amongst those pigeons. Sorry I had to tell a deliberate lie to the old girl, Shiner, but I wanted to leave no doubt about it. God! Life's going to be thunder and lightning in that kitchen for the next hour or two. But that's the only thing that'll help us. When the family's exploded, we can go round and pick up the pieces."

"You think one of them did it?"

"Bugger it!"

Kenworthy had just reeled sideways from a narrow trodden track and side-stepped up to his knee in a drift.

"If it wasn't one of the family, then it was either someone who was lurking about near the tree, or who had just arrived at the moment the girl left the house. The former is a possibility, but if it was someone looking for the cache, he'd left it a bit late. If it was a local, in the know, he'd have come days earlier. So that leaves the casual caller, someone who followed her to the tree, had an altercation, got the gun, perhaps took it out of her own hand, and shot her. That would be a coincidence—never to be discounted, Shiner— and never to be seized in both hands whilst more likely alternatives remain to be tidied up."

They walked twenty heavy yards in silence. It seemed harder work going downhill than the climbing had been.

"It narrows it down to two," Wright said.

"It narrows it down to two. Emily we can discount, and Pollard too, I'm pretty sure."

"What worries me, sir, is the limit of this family loyalty business. I can understand them sticking together to cover up for Calverley's one night of love . . ."

"It's a psychological point that I'm not competent to answer, Shiner. If Calverley did it, then I think his mother would go to any length to protect him. The Pollards could easily be taken in tow—at least, in the initial stages. But if Edith did it, would Calverley cover up for her? I doubt it, Shiner, I very much doubt it."

"Of course, he'd go to any length to avoid a scandal."

"And swing it onto Booth, you mean, whatever poison he had in his heart for Edith? A bit far-fetched. Of course, it wouldn't take them ten seconds to declare Booth expendable. But God, Shiner, the man would have to have a heart of concrete."

"And hasn't he?"

"I doubt it. We shall know tonight. When he comes to see us in an hour or two, as he will, of his own volition, we shall learn infinitely more about him than we know at present."

They reached the gate at which they had paused for second wind on their way up, and stopped again to look at the view. There was an unnatural stillness in the trees and roof-tops, as if the whole scene was waiting in suspended animation for the grey of the early winter evening to absorb it.

"What do you make of Lady Edith?" Wright asked. "For sheer, cold, unadulterated bloody nastiness——"

"We might *have* to psycho-analyse her, Shiner, or that might turn out to be a luxury for which we can't afford the time. And we might fail, at that. We certainly might fail."

"I'd certainly like to see how you'd set about it!"

Kenworthy smiled genuinely, as if he were actually pleased with the compliment.

"Complete emotional collapse, that would have to be the first step. It might have to be contrived artificially, but my guess is that it'll happen spontaneously anyway, within the next few days. Damn it, Shiner, she can't hold out for ever. And when reaction does come, it's going to be pretty deep-dyed."

"All of which is rather a complicated definition of the word *bitch*."

"Bitch? Oh, yes, she's a bitch. First generation of this family to go respectable. That demands bitchiness, for a start. How she must have hated this background, looking back at it from the lofty heights of the lower middle class. How'd you like to be married to her, Shiner?"

"Somebody must have loved her."

"And there's no need for me to repeat the old one about looking at the mantelpiece."

"She must have led her husband a dog's life."

"But you've got to admit, Shiner, she's produced a brigade major, a college tutor, an M.P. and undoubtedly, sooner or later, a cabinet minister."

"But has she produced a man?"

"On the evidence of yesterday's post mortem, yes."

"It's taken him long enough."

"All part of the picture, and I don't mean the image. Can't you imagine what sort of a boyhood he must have had, Shiner? Taught not to say boo to geese? Held to his books and probably not even allowed to go to the cinema? Missed Rin Tin Tin and Buck Jones. Certainly sheltered from girls, as from anything else that might have deflected him. Hence the first time he saw one in the flesh, he was stymied. Remember? He couldn't even talk to his cousin when he had a swotting holiday here."

"He made up for that last week."

"Shiner, you've been seeing too much of me. I do believe I'm turning you into a cynic. And that would be a pity. Let's go home. I'm bloody cold."

They tramped down through the snow, conversation impossible, as they were unable to walk abreast. But when they reached the road opposite the Volunteer, Wright began again to press the argument.

"You say he couldn't say boo to a goose. I've never moved in the company of brigade majors, but I've always understood they said a damned sight more than boo to lieutenant-colonels and the like."

"From behind the brigadier's skirts."

"But he led a controversial existence as a college tutor."

"Sheltering behind a college name and several hundred years of tradition."

"And as an M.P., holding office already."

"Backed by the parliamentary and political machine."

"You're saying, in fact, that he doesn't do things on his own initiative?"

"I'm saying he's a bloody good staff officer. But that's not real leadership; it's only training for it. Nobody's ever cast off Calverley's moorings yet. His mother doesn't even think the umbilical cord's gone. When she made him come up to this funeral, it was to act as *her* staff officer. And that's a bit of knowledge that might be very helpful to us before we've finished."

"It's obvious he's going to be a bit of a handful when it comes to the show-down."

"And that will be this evening, Shiner. I think we can depend upon it."

✦ 10 ✦

KENWORTHY SPREAD OUT his papers to cover every square inch of the table: manilla folders, the statements that Judson had taken, and what appeared to be reams of summarized evidence in his own tiny, crowded handwriting. This was an activity of the superintendent's that Wright had never witnessed before. Kenworthy's filing system normally seemed to be incorporated in his brain, and he affected an almost pathological distaste for pen and paper. Yet it now looked as if he must have worked well into the night. There were sketch plans of the village and a layout of the farm in black indian ink, and even the clippings from the gossip column had been pasted onto sheets of paper with copious footnotes and marginalia.

"Just for once," he said, "I want Calverley, when he calls, to think I've actually done some work on this case."

There were sounds of booted feet crossing the floor of the adjoining bar.

"You'd better go and keep the intelligentsia company, Shiner. You might possibly pick something up. But don't drink too much. I want Calverley to get a startling picture of cold efficiency. And the moment he does come in, leave the bar and come in here, with your notebook at the ready. I want every word down, even the side-chat. A couple of sentences might sew this thing up, and there's every chance that they may be spoken within the next two hours."

Wright left him to his stacked paper work and went into the public room. The noisy boots had belonged to Ben Drabble, and the Water Board man was the only drinker. Isaac Pennington was almost opposite him, with his elbows on the bar, and neither of them was speaking. At the sight of the sergeant, the landlord's hand went to the handle of his bitter beer pump, but Wright shook his head.

"Better have something soft, I think. What have you got, bitter lemon?"

Ben Drabble scarcely looked at him. After about a minute, he pushed his half-finished beer away and asked for a double whisky. Pennington seemed surprised, but obviously did not want to show it.

"Trying to thaw yourself out, Ben?"

Drabble drank greedily of the neat spirit, finishing two-thirds of it in one draught.

"Never been so bloody cold in my life," he said.

"Wouldn't have your job for a hundred quid a week, in this weather," Pennington consoled him.

"The dam's in a bloody mess, Isaac. I've managed to get one out-fall clear. But you'd need dynamite in numbers four and five."

"It can't last for ever," Pennington said.

Drabble poured the rest of his whisky into his beer and turned to Wright.

"Your boss said a right bloody thing last night. About the old days. About old Thomas John killing young Margaret when he chucked that stone sixty years ago. I've had a horrible bloody day—a horrible bloody day. Stuck on my own, for hours on end in those bloody culverts. Horrible bloody thoughts kept coming into my head. And do you know what one of them was? It suddenly struck me it was as if the old man had got into the ice. And I reckon he bloody has, too."

Wright and Kenworthy had looked on Drabble, since they had first set foot in this bar, as the spokesman of Carrion Clough's superstitions. It had seemed partially jocular at first, amusing, naïve: the yokels unable to adjust themselves to the violence of events. Then it had begun to become boring. One knew what everyone was going to say, and there was no point in arguing with it. But now there was a new element in it: fear as cold as the ice in the out-falls. Ben Drabble was frightened to the depths of his marrow.

Even Isaac Pennington, who asked no more than that his customers should be unruffled, was infected by it.

"Nay, lad, you're letting it get you down. Have another whisky—on the house."

The whisky appeared, but Drabble seemed not to notice it.

"There was nothing but bad came from Moss Hill Farm," he said, "and we haven't seen the last of it yet."

Then Anthony Calverley came in, bulky, brisk, but subdued.

"Is your superintendent available, please?"

Wright picked up his drink, taking care that the bitter lemon bottle was clearly noted, and opened the door for Calverley to precede him into the sitting-room.

Kenworthy looked up without surprise from his tidy piles of paper. He had evidently been up to his room, for he was sitting now with his old blue dressing-gown girdled tightly over his suit.

"I owe you an apology, Superintendent, well, both of you, of course."

He treated Wright to a thin smile which, even if it was tailor-made for the fleeting instant, was nevertheless a show of humanity.

"Of course, I know you have a duty to do. I know you have a scientific approach to these things, and you have to be cold-blooded, in the face of all types. And you have to put on an act—may I call for drinks for us, gentlemen?"

"By all means have anything you'd like for yourself. The sergeant and I would prefer to abstain for the time being."

Kenworthy still had his open fountain-pen poised in his fingers.

"I've come to offer my help," Calverley said. "All the help I can. After all, I'm not entirely devoid of intelligence, and I do realize that there is a certain accumulation of evidence."

"Which incriminates you and your mother?"

"Oh, for goodness' sake, Superintendent, leave my mother out of this. I know what sort of impression she must have created, but you can't possibly know her as she is. Anything further out of character . . ."

"Mr. Calverley, as far as motivation, opportunity and circumstantial evidence are concerned, I could build up a case against your mother every whit as damning as the case against yourself."

And this Kenworthy proceeded to do, coolly, courteously and factually, taking Calverley, to Wright's surprise, into close confidence about his theories.

"There's only one thing I feel certain about, Mr. Calverley: I'm sure the pair of you didn't collaborate before the fact. But how much collusion there's been since is still food for thought. I said to Sergeant Wright this afternoon: she'd co-operate to cover you up, but I think you'd draw the line at covering up for her."

Calverley was taken aback.

"Superintendent Kenworthy, I know this all looks desperately black. And I'm grateful to you for not hiding any nuance of how your mind has been working. But at rock-bottom you must *know*——"

"Let's talk about your mother first, shall we?"

"What can I say? You're not likely to be affected by protestations, however vigorous."

"It might help if we could begin to understand her hatred for your cousin. That's something you can't deny. It's a talking point in the whole village. And amongst your own family."

Calverley breathed deeply. "This unfortunately is true. My mother has always hated Margaret. Look, do you mind if I do go and get myself a drink? Are you sure you won't join me?"

He went into the bar.

"Strong self-discipline," Kenworthy said softly. "Let's hope he keeps it up. It wouldn't take much for him to crack, and I'd not like that to happen, till I'm ready for it."

Calverley came back with a large whiskey, pale from a liberal lacing with soda.

"If you want to understand my mother, Superintendent, you'll have to go a good way back into the past."

"As with other aspects of this case."

"The key to her character is that she herself had a mother-fixation. It's curious, you know: I've known this for years. Yet this is the first time I've ever put it into words."

"A mother fixation," Kenworthy prompted.

"Yes. Not surprising, really. You must have put together a pretty vivid picture of what my grandfather was like— what sort of life he wished on his family. But my grandmother was such a gentle soul. She suffered so much, and so serenely. I expect it was for the sake of her children."

"She was a local woman?"

"No. She came from East Anglia. When she was a girl she came into service at Warburton Hall, ultimately became the cook. A beautiful cook she was, too. Curiously enough, that was why Margaret was still doing the laundry for the Hall. It was a family association that had gone on through the generations. I said to Margaret, when she didn't want me to help her carry the basket, "If it was good enough for my grandmother, it's good enough for me.""

Calverley sipped his drink.

"My grandfather lost no time in discovering her. There was a whirlwind courtship—village fairgrounds, and all that sort of thing. He was a young tough, and undoubtedly a bit of a gallant, when he wanted to turn it on. Then there was a penniless marriage. My great-grandfather didn't hold with the match. He settled a hovel on them in the old village, paid him a menial wage for menial tasks: dry-stone walling and the like. My mother was conceived the night the old man came back from South Africa—I expect you've heard about that in there."

He jerked his head in the direction of the bar.

"After that there was a rapprochement between my grandfather and his father. They worked together on these deals in real estate. Again, you'll have heard the gory details."

"The bitterness isn't over yet."

"There was nothing dishonest about it," Calverley said. "But by the standards of the age and place, their bargaining must have been pretty aggressive. They upset a lot of people—who'd have been upset anyway, when the reservoir came. Damn it, we have the same problem today, with new towns, overspill, slum clearance and sonic boom."

Kenworthy smiled. "Thank you for reminding me that we're still in the twentieth century."

"I doubt whether Carrion Clough is. At any rate, the old

man made his pile. And my reading of his character is that he was secretly too ashamed ever to use it. But he moved the family up to the Moss Hill Farm—the only habitable small-holding left in the whole of the gathering grounds, mark you, and that didn't help public relations. Anyway, my mother was born. The youngest: and, I think my grand-mother was determined, the last. I've often wondered what she thought when she let him make love to her, that night, after those empty years. He'd cleared off and left her, you know, without a word, for the length of the war. With two children, and virtually no income, in a hovel. She didn't spoil my mother. She was too shrewd for that. But my mother was the apple of her eye. It's twenty years since she died, but my mother hasn't recovered from it yet."

"And Margaret?"

"Margaret took over the running of the farm. Lock, stock and barrel. Primed the pump on frosty days with a little old saucepan my grandmother had always used; basted the joint with grandma's ladle; used grandma's pastry-board, her irons, her armchair. And she was meticulously loyal to grand-dad. My mother couldn't stand it. I know it isn't reasonable."

"It's reasonable enough as a starting-point," Kenworthy said. "And there are other things. Your mother expected you to have a mother-fixation, too, didn't she? Perhaps you have."

Calverley studied him coldly for some seconds. Wright wondered whether Kenworthy might be pressing his luck. But the moment passed. Calverley contained himself.

"I haven't. But I've always done my best to treat her as she's hoped I'd treat her."

"Good for you! But then there's the point that she knew—perhaps a good deal earlier than you knew yourself—that you were in love with your cousin."

"What are you getting at?"

"You came here for a holiday—to study—when you were eighteen."

Calverley actually blushed. "You fancy yourself as a psychiatrist, don't you?" he said. "If you'd put as much effort into the things that matter, this case would have been solved by now."

He said it without bitterness, and certainly not provocatively, but he was emphatic nevertheless.

"You've been in love with your cousin since you were eighteen. You know now that that's true."

"And irrelevant."

"Not irrelevant. Because twenty-five years ago, you didn't face the facts. But I'll bet your mother did."

"So?"

"So, seeing the way things have moved since you came up here a week or more ago, we can now provide her with a clinically perfect motive."

"Feasible. And fatuous."

Kenworthy transferred a thin, clipped sheaf of his notes from one pile to another, then sat back and smiled pleasantly.

"I'm inclined to agree with you. I don't think she did it. But I'm glad we've talked it out, all the same. We can always come back to it if need be. Let's move now, in similar vein, to the case against yourself."

"Not until you've answered a fundamental question for me first."

"Anything you like."

"Have you eliminated Booth? And if so, on what grounds?"

Kenworthy explained the circumstances in which P.C. Russell had come into the hen-house. Hitherto the details had not been divulged.

Calverley took the point, but he pondered it carefully.

"Booth heard the shot, did he, as well as Russell?"

"He says so."

"How much reliance can you place on that? Booth is highly suggestible."

"You can say that again."

"And if you put him in as a Crown witness, I hope I'm there to see it."

"That's what I said to Sergeant Wright."

"Has it occurred to you that the man who's come out of this with the neatest alibi is Russell himself?"

"It has."

"And you know, of course—you're bound to have delved into this—that Russell fancied his chances with my cousin?"

"We know that, too. What we don't know is how strong his chances were."

"Nil," Calverley said. "I can tell you that categorically—and there's no wishful thinking in it."

"Don't forget that after the funeral, your cousin was going to be a free agent for the first time in her life."

"Very true. And she knew what she was going to do with herself. She was going to China."

"China?"

"Shakes you, doesn't it? Thank God I know something you don't. And *I* didn't believe it either—at first."

Calverley paused. Kenworthy reached for a fresh sheet of paper.

"You'd better fill me in."

"It won't help your case-work."

"Everything helps my case-work."

Calverley took more whisky. For a moment it seemed as if he were going to retreat and decline to talk. Then, still unusually red about the cheeks, he began, bringing in more and more extraneous detail as he grew accustomed to sharing confidences with the policemen. It was as if—and this must surely be true—he had had no chance for days, perhaps for weeks and months, to talk to any man who might understand what was in his mind.

Wright stole a glance at Kenworthy. The superintendent was sitting politely expectant, with all the disciplined kindliness of a father confessor. Ready at any moment to arrest the man for murder, perhaps on the turn of an equivocal phrase, he nevertheless had Calverley in the palm of his hand: probably the cleverest and potentially the most awkward customer he had ever interrogated.

Calverley looked askance at Wright's notebook and pencil.

"He's not going to write *this* down, is he?"

Kenworthy signalled with his eyes. Wright laid his writing materials aside.

"I'm well aware that I don't come out of this very well. The way I treated Margaret when I was a student—well, you can form your own opinion about it. Actually, I could make a case out for it. I think in some ways I was suffering from arrested development."

"Don't be too hard on yourself," Kenworthy said. "You'd had an unnatural boyhood, for which, in some ways, you now have certain reasons to be grateful."

"As maybe. But I didn't spare a thought for the effect it might have had on Margaret."

"She remembered, did she?"

"I behaved worse than badly. Even sent her an annual Christmas card, with the House of Commons crest on it. Pure self-glorification. This has left me with no illusions about myself. I'm telling you this so that you can get an honest picture. If, when I've finished, you still think I could have killed her, you're welcome to lose your reputation on it."

"You'd gone on hurting her for more than twenty years?"

"She was more perceptive than anyone can imagine. And outspoken. 'A card with a portcullis on it,' she called it. I can tell you, things were pretty sticky when I first came up here—it seems months ago. And my mother made things worse, all along the line. Insisting that she always prefaced my Christian name with *Cousin*, and that sort of nonsense."

"You didn't stand out against it?"

Calverley pulled a face.

"Don't make me more disgusted with myself than I am already. I was all for the quiet life. I suppose I thought I could get away with it for ever. Margaret treated me better than I deserved. Kept me at more than arm's length, treated me to some bitter sarcasm in the few odd moments we were alone together. But she was prepared to wait on me hand and foot: till after the funeral. She was a girl who made herself targets—just as she had always determined she would look after the old man to the bitter end. And whatever was happening in the house, I could feel that she was weighing it all up, seeing through me. God, Carrion Clough has been a catharsis! I'd tried to dodge coming here in the first instance, then I let my mother prevail. That was the iron that had entered into Felicity Urquhart's bloody little soul."

Kenworthy's fingers moved quietly towards one of the sheets to which the newspaper cuttings were pasted, and edged it towards him on the table.

"And I was determined I wouldn't stay in that house at any cost. I'd booked by phone at the Legless Volunteer. But again my mother won the day. There was a horrible scene about it, particularly since I'd had the temerity to eat a meal at the pub before going up to the farm. And Margaret had been keeping a pie in the oven. That was the first time I'd

seen her again after all these years. I could feel her eyes in
the background, seeing the truth under everything, saying
nothing. And there was a row about my grandfather's box,
almost before I was in the house. My mother called on me
to bully my cousin."

"Which you did?"

"No. That, to my credit, I can honestly say. I just
half-heartedly asked her what had happened to it, then
dropped the matter. To my mother's fury. And it was after
that that my cousin and I first came together alone. Oh,
nothing happened. It's not worth telling. My mother insisted
that my car ought to be put under cover. But there was an
odd old dray in the only shed that would serve. It had to be
shifted, and it hadn't been moved for years. Margaret came
out to help me with it, in the dark, with a silk scarf tied
round her head, because it was beginning to snow. I
remember barking my shins against an old rat trap that was
hanging on the wall. And I couldn't get the thing to budge.
Then Margaret stooped down and picked up a half-brick
that was buried in the loose soil under one of the wheels. A
couple of seconds later she had the shafts under her elbows
and had pulled the thing out single-handed. She had the
strength of an ox, you know. Then she ran across the yard
in front of me, held the door for me, laughing—but you
know what I mean: not unkindly this time."

Kenworthy went to the fireplace and tapped out his pipe.
Wright did not move a limb.

"There was more trouble when we got indoors. Still about
the box. My mother wanted to get it settled before the
Pollards arrived. It got so damned unpleasant that I left the
house. Made an excuse of wanting to come down here and
telephone my Minister. Which was true, anyway. Only I
stayed, and drank a good deal more than was good for me.

And joined in all the stupid talk: my grandfather's death has had an effect on every man in this village, you know."

"You must have been talking to Ben Drabble."

"When I got back, my mother had gone to bed. Mercifully. Margaret was still up, unusually for her, because she was normally in bed by nine. Always up at five. And she was worried, because I was soaked to the skin. The snow had come on pretty heavily whilst I'd been swilling beer. She got a bowl of scalding hot water, and put half a tin of mustard powder in it, and made me soak my feet. Old folks' remedy. And when I flinched, she bent down and held my ankles, so there was no escape. That's how we started talking. And that's when we broke through the barrier of mistrust and hurtfulness for the first time."

He stopped to look at their faces and see how they were taking it. Kenworthy looked directly into his eyes.

"She had a pile of about half a dozen books on a corner of the table: she'd started clearing up her belongings, as it were. And I could see she was anxious for me to ask about them, so I did. And she'd got a passion for China. She showed me one: a Band of Hope prize her father had won for a temperance essay. Superficial stuff: line-drawings of opium smokers, a criminal with a damned great board round his neck, cormorant fishers. You know the sort of thing. Then she said she was going to China, when the farm had been sold. The old man had left her pretty well provided for. I played along with her a bit, told her that this wasn't the ideal game and age for tourism in Outer Mongolia."

Calverley was still flushed. It was doing him good to resurrect the details.

"But she said she didn't want to be a tourist. She wanted to work amongst the people. Gladys Aylward had managed it—why shouldn't she? And she asked me to use my good offices to find a channel for her. I had to flannel a bit: didn't want to let her down too badly. It was only slowly dawning on me how serious she was about it. I'm beginning to think now, if other things had worked out differently, that she might have had a try. But all I could do was extemporize. Said I'd dig around."

"Which didn't impress her?"

"No, it didn't. She saw through me. And then I started to tell her that China these days is a very different proposition from a late-nineteenth-century school-book. That was where she rounded on me. Asked me if I thought I had all the brains in the family. And by God, what she knew about China was nobody's business. There's a County Library van comes up here once a week. She'd asked for a reading programme, over seven or eight years. She could lose me on the cultural revolution and the entourage of Chairman Mao. I deferred to her, and made her promise she'd have a holiday in London with me, before she took a boat. And that's a long story, but you know now why she wasn't interested in P.C. Russell."

"Which wouldn't stop P.C. Russell being interested in her."

"All I'm saying is that there was nothing firm between them."

Was Calverley still feeling slightly jealous of the constable?

Kenworthy changed the subject abruptly.

"What made you so certain that she'd gone up to that burnt-out tree?" he asked.

"You mean that the speed with which I followed her is the most damning piece of evidence against me?"

"I mean: how did you know where she'd gone?"

Calverley tilted his glass and contemplated it for a few seconds.

"It's easy to know, not so easy to explain. It would hold no water at all in a court of law. She went there to pray. At least, not to pray in the conventional sense of the word. That tree was a symbol in Margaret's life. It had been since she was in her teens. She used to go there to think, to make her mind up about things, to—what's the word?—re-dedicate herself. Look at it fairly and squarely, Superintendent, she'd had a hell of a life. She was hard-headed. With a bit of schooling she could have been brainy within the meaning of the act. But there was also a good deal of the primitive about her. There *had* to be, don't you see? That tree was not exactly a fetish, but it was getting on that way. You'll find a certain atmosphere of throw-back in the gathering grounds, Superintendent."

"That's putting it mildly," Kenworthy said.

"Don't get the impression that *I* belong here."

"You belong here more closely than you think. And why should she have wanted to go and pray, or think, or moon about, or whatever it was, on this occasion?"

"You know very well the answer to that. My mother had just insulted her abominably."

"I haven't heard *you* say so."

"But you know what happened. You've dug it out in your devastating way. My mother had just called her a filthy name."

"Why?"

"You know why. Can't we take this as read?"

"I shall have to hear your version sooner or later. Maybe in more forbidding circumstances than this."

Calverley finished his whisky, but he made no move to go and have his glass replenished.

"I'd better go back a bit in time. On the morning of the day on which all this happened, I'd motored down into Cotter Bridge. Partly to see old Horncastle about coming up to read the will; partly to put the affair of my grandfather's box into the hands of the police."

"On your mother's insistence?"

"Let's say that she had a *prima facie* case. There *was* a box. It was known about in the village as well as in the family. It contained my grandfather's fortune; and God knows what or what not that was worth. But it had gone. There were marks on the lino and against the skirting board of his bedroom where it had stood for sixty years. Margaret insisted that he had given it to her, years ago—yes, long enough to have established it as a deed of gift. He'd told her that when he went, the box and its contents were hers. She made no bones about the fact that she'd disposed of it. She would not say what she had done with it."

"And whose side were you on? Both?"

"No. I'd have fought to the last ditch for her right to every penny he'd left. But, naturally, I wanted it to be legal and above board."

"So she knew why you were going to Cotter Bridge?"

"Not perhaps in so many words."

"Did she or didn't she?"

"She did."

"So up to and including your trip to Cotter Bridge police-station, you were, in point of fact, playing your mother's game against her?"

Calverley was uncomfortable. A lesser man might have wriggled in his seat.

"I was trying to compromise."

"I'll bet that isn't how Margaret looked on it. I should have thought she'd have treated you with complete contempt."

The interrogation had taken on a fresh turn. Kenworthy was putting on the pressure. But Calverley was being deliberately unruffled.

"That's what I'm coming to. I stayed in Cotter Bridge for lunch. I had some of that blasted horseradish sauce you talked about. By the time I'd driven back it was late afternoon, getting dark, still snowing, utterly primeval and miserable. As I passed this pub I saw Margaret, with this enormous wicker washing-basket on her hip, walking towards the reservoir. I stopped and tried to offer her a lift, but she wouldn't accept. She was too angry with me, too independent. I drove slowly, alongside her, stopping every few yards, all the way to the bank-side. In the end, I prevailed on her to get in."

"How?"

"Talked sense into her. I don't want you to be mistaken, Superintendent, about what our relationship was. She was furious with me, and was very, very proud of her self-sufficiency. But I think we understood one another. Earlier on I'd told her I was going to come out in the open and side with her against my mother. She pleaded with me not to. She said I'd got to go on living with her, and she hadn't. She was inconsistent, of course. But surely that makes sense?"

Kenworthy tapped the newspaper cutting with the tips of his fingers.

"And who saw her get into your car?"

Calverley shrugged his shoulders.

"It was snowing hard. I wasn't paying much attention to my surroundings. Anyone might have been about."

"Wilfred Wilson, for example."

"I certainly didn't see him. The only person I did see was Drabble, the waterman, coming up from his dam, knocking off for the day. But I discount him. He's not the sort to write letters to the press. And even if he did pen one, they'd surely not accept his evidence unsupported. I mean, even the chap who edits Felix's column must make *some* concessions to prudence. Now look here, Superintendent, I wouldn't have thought, in a case like this, you'd have had any difficulty at all in getting the facts from the newspaper."

"You don't know the press."

"If you can find out who inspired that milk-maid item, you've got the man who murdered my cousin."

"A highly unscientific remark, if I may say so. But I'll admit I'd like to know. In fact, I intend to know. But for the moment . . ."

"We drove towards the Hall. An insane proposition, I can now see. And Margaret did warn me. Unmade lanes, up across the moors. So much drifting that there was no hope of seeing what was road, what was banks of heather, or what was gully. I was mad. I was mad with Carrion Clough, I was mad with my mother. I was very anxious to put things right with Margaret. And I was determined to get that car there by willpower if necessary. We ended up in a gully."

"And spent the night there."

"There was nothing else for it. If we'd tried to walk in the dark, we could have gone over a precipice in any one of a hundred places. But that's not an excuse. I'm not ashamed of what happened. I've got it straight in my own mind now and——"

Kenworthy nodded. "When did you get back home?"

"By midday the next day. We'd had to dig our way out of the car. It was the very devil of an operation. And then it was a long, difficult and dangerous walk. It was also rather a lovely one."

"And you came home to a somewhat sticky reception?"

"Tight-lipped. My mother just wouldn't speak. But there was so much to do, getting out of wet clothes. A hip-bath, with all that that entailed in an overcrowded little house like that. My mother wouldn't speak, all through lunch. But she was also intensely curious as to what exactly had happened. We started talking in the afternoon, and she prised some of the facts from us. It probably wasn't difficult for her to deduce the rest. Margaret and I decided that we were going to do our best to see that the peace was kept till after the funeral. But it must have been apparent to anybody what we felt about each other. I know my aunt Emily saw it, because she took me on one side in the kitchen and said she was happy for us, and it would all work out. Then, later in the afternoon, my mother broke down and insulted Margaret to the ends of the earth. Margaret just couldn't take it. She ran out."

"And is it true that you hung back, arguing with your mother, before you went after her?"

"For perhaps half a minute. Does it seem so difficult to understand? My mother was hysterical. I was trying to shout some sense into her."

"Did you actually open the door?"

"And closed it again. We'd have had a snow-drift in the kitchen."

"What was your first reaction when you heard the shot?"

"I thought she'd shot herself."

"That's not in character, surely?"

"Revolver shots in Carrion Clough are not in character."

"Did you know the revolver was hidden in the tree?"

"Yes. Margaret had told me. She'd got it out of the house as soon as the old man died. She was going to throw it into the reservoir at the first opportunity. She'd hated the thing all her life."

"When you heard the shot, you rushed out?"

"Obviously."

"And you got rid of your uncle by sending him to look in the outhouses?"

"That's true."

"You didn't see any sign that anyone else had come up to the farm?"

"It was too dark. The snow was too thick. I was too preoccupied."

Kenworthy toyed with his papers for some seconds.

"You realize that that thirty-second delay before you went out into the blizzard is your only hope of proving your innocence?"

At some stage in the last few minutes, Calverley had lost his colour. White-faced, he spoke with quiet honesty.

"I appreciate that that's how it must look to a policeman."

"Or a jury. And that if this murder was not committed by a member of your family, it must have been the handiwork of someone who had arrived on the scene at the precise moment when your cousin left the house?"

"Or who had arrived earlier, and was lurking, waiting his opportunity."

Kenworthy looked up sharply.

"Have you any specific reason for suggesting that, Mr. Calverley?"

"None at all. It seems to be the only reasonable alternative."

"Not very reasonable at all, if I may say so, Mr. Calverley. Lurking? In a storm such as you've described? Wouldn't such a visitor have lurked in an outhouse? And didn't your uncle account for the outhouses?"

"*After* the shot," Calverley said.

"You've gone into this pretty thoroughly, haven't you?"

"Wouldn't you have done? Do you think I've thought of anything else since?"

"At what stage did you decide to compound a lie about the reason for your cousin's distress?"

Kenworthy picked up a sheaf of statements.

"I suppose those have got to come to light," Calverley said.

"If anything comes to light, everything's got to come to light. At what stage, Mr. Calverley?"

"We had a family conference that evening."

"Who made the decision?"

"My mother and I."

"Why?"

"The reason's obvious."

"Nothing's obvious. Why?"

"There was no point in muck-raking, Superintendent. We

did not see that it could affect the issue. I still have my life to lead."

He did not want to say more on the theme. He waited for Kenworthy's rejoinder, and Kenworthy did not hurry to oblige him.

"We're a long way from Whitehall, Mr. Calverley," he said at last.

"A very long way."

"I only hope you make your way back there."

"You're still reluctant to accept my account of myself. But I've been very honest with you, Superintendent. I've said a good deal more than I intended to when I came into the room."

"I'd like to accept it, Mr. Calverley. But you can see that there remains a lot more work for me to do."

"I am at your disposal, if I can help. I mean, in investigation, too. There may be people who'd talk to me who wouldn't talk to you.

Could anything, Wright thought, be further from the truth? The man was intelligent, accustomed to command, but had he any of the warmth of humanity about him?

"I shall know where to find you," Kenworthy said, and then, when Calverley had left them, "Well, Shiner?"

"I believe him. I think I'm beginning to understand the man, and to like him."

"But that isn't exactly what we've come here for, is it?"

"Only indirectly."

Kenworthy bundled his documents roughly together, as if he had no further use for them.

"If the Calverley's didn't do it, we've more or less got to start again, haven't we?"

"That's true, sir."

"I might have to push Calverley, yet. It may be the only way of finding out what there really is in him. And after all, we *are* a long way from Whitehall."

✦ 11 ✦

P.C. RUSSELL WAS at the Legless Volunteer the next morning whilst the Londoners were still in the expansive second half of their breakfast.

"Cup of tea?" Kenworthy asked, almost aggressively, as if to assert that he was not prepared to discuss work for another ten minutes.

Fresh-faced, boyishly eager, Russell was wearing pressed flannels under a leather-buttoned trench-coat. He leaned two pairs of improvised snow-shoes against the wall of the parlour.

"Think they're going to work, Constable?"

"I've tried them out, sir. It's slow going, and they're not infallible in the powdery stuff. But they should enable us to get to some places we couldn't otherwise reach."

"Well, that's where you're going, Constable—places you couldn't otherwise reach."

To Wright's surprise, Kenworthy forewent the three or four extra slices of toast to which he usually indulged himself.

"I've got work to do, Shiner. Don't spend half the morning here."

He went upstairs, and a minute or two later let himself out through the front door.

Wright felt as if the mantle of Kenworthy had descended upon him, and took unexcited pleasure in the process. He called Martha Pennington for an extra cup and saucer, and made Russell draw a chair up to the table."

"There's no need for us to rush at it. And we may as well do our talking here as out in the bloody cold."

Kenworthy, too, would have started off by gently deflating this young man's ballooning enthusiasm. And there was little doubt, from the light in Russell's eyes, and from the way in which he failed to make himself comfortable in his chair, that this was to be the greatest day in the constable's life.

"We're going up to the Hall?" he asked.

"To begin with. And I'd like to know all you can tell me about the people up there."

"Pump him," Kenworthy had said. "Chatter like bloody magpies. Take him over the ground we already know. Because he ought to know Carrion Clough better than any man in the village—even Wilfred Wilson."

"Commander Brayshaw. I couldn't say I knew him well, you know. Naval family. Have been for generations."

"And there was a long tradition of service between the Halliwells and the Brayshaws?"

"That's right—gentry."

"We're inclined to think that they may be able to help us about the third newspaper cutting—the one about the milk-maid. There are so few people around here who might have done it. Do you think it could possibly have been the Brayshaws? Would it be in character?"

Russell hesitated too long. The question was too difficult for him. He did not know the Brayshaws well enough.

"Take him into your confidence," Kenworthy had urged. *"Don't be afraid to let him know all we know, and all we're thinking. We're so far out on a limb that it can't make any odds."*

"It's important," Wright said. "Kenworthy thinks that the authorship of that press leak could be the clue to the whole issue."

Russell held his features very firm, and did not reply at once.

"I'm afraid it's a bit out of my ken," he said.

"Don't forget that he remains a major suspect. Your job, Shiner, is to play him both ways. And I'm leaving it to you because you'll do it better than me. You're nearer to him than I am."

"Yes, well, it is a bit of a fast ball," Wright said. "A mystery within a mystery. We *shall* get to the bottom of it."

He finished his tea, and Russell hurried to do the same.

"You might find it a sound plan just to let him know, casually, now and then, that he isn't entirely in the clear."

But Wright thought it a little early in the day for that. They pulled the tops of their socks over the turn-ups of their trousers, and Russell showed him how to fix the snow-shoes, a complicated and back-breaking business.

"I feel a proper bloody nana in these," Wright said, as they walked towards the wall of the reservoir.

"We shouldn't stand a chance without them. I'm not at all that sure that we stand a chance with them."

Wright turned into Dick Haines's shop to stock up with cigarettes; and Kenworthy was leaning over the counter, poring over a small pile of picture postcards.

"Here we are—at last! Haven't sent the wife a genuine Old Master since we left Cotter Bridge. Look at this one."

It was a matt, sepia photograph of the reservoir, dating from the nineteen twenties at the latest, and showing the waters at their lowest summer ebb, with the top of the church steeple plainly visible, and even the gaping gable of a submerged barn.

"I'll have half a dozen of these," Kenworthy said, and then he caught sight of the contraptions on his colleagues' feet and roared with unkind laughter.

"Well, well, well! If the rations run out, you can always shoot a husky."

"It was your bloody idea," Wright told him.

They had to cross the dam and then follow what Wright assumed was normally a narrow track leading steeply up into the moorlands. Only it was impossible to tell where the track ended and its deeply banked sides began, for the snow in its drifting had added a completely new contour to the landscape, turning hollows into sharply ridged dunes, and in others dipping in windswept bowls over ground that was actually rising. Fortunately Russell's knowledge of the terrain was intimate, though there were times when he led them yards astray and had to stop to seek bearings from landmarks that seemed to have been diabolically changed in shape and position.

And although the snow-shoes made the trek possible, they did not make it easy. One had to lift one's feet so very high in order to put them down again level, that it would have been gruelling physical labour even on the flat. And until one got used to balancing the things, they had a habit of digging into the snow rim first, which not only frustrated their purpose, but involved constant halts for extrication.

"I still think she was mad to think of walking up here with her basket," Wright said.

"She stood a reasonable chance while the storm was in its early stages. It's the drifting afterwards that's made it like

this. I'd sooner have done it on foot than in a car—
especially a big car."

"Of course, he must have driven up here, mustn't he?"

The natural gradient where they were standing must have
been one in five.

"Bloody crazy," Wright said.

Once Russell stopped, listening carefully, and side-
stepped through a gap in a broken grit-stone wall.

"Look at this poor bastard!"

A sheep had become trapped at the bottom of a drift and
was alive only because the warmth of its breath had melted
airholes through a yard of snow. Russell brought the two
halves of an army entrenching tool from the pockets of his
raincoat and began to put them together.

"What are you going to do?"

"Dig the poor sod out."

"Sorry, mate. On our way back, if there's time."

Russell looked momentarily hurt.

"Suppose you're right," he said. "We'll have to organize
a helicopter lift to feed them. We did that the winter after the
war."

They reached a point at which they had to take a sharp
turn to the left, and it took Russell several false starts to find
the track he wanted, which mercifully ceased to climb and
began to follow a lateral ridge of the hill-side. But after they
had rounded a scarp, they came to a stretch in the lee of the
slope where the going was easier. They stopped and took
stock of their surroundings.

They were now moving parallel to the reservoir, but two
or three hundred feet above it. To their left the ground fell
away in a sheer drop, and it was clear from the lie of the
snow that they were overlooking the strewn boulders of a
disused quarry.

"I can understand why they didn't risk walking home at night."

Russell grunted.

"The swine!" he said.

Wright needed to remember that Russell had been in love with Margaret, that the night in the car was something to which he had not yet adjusted himself. He said no more for the time being.

An hour later, they reached Warburton Hall, a dour grey-stone manor built to endure anything that the elements of the gathering grounds could offer it.

The bell-pull operated a rusty, creaking wire, and an elderly, comfortably built housekeeper asked them in.

"I'm afraid Commander and Mrs. Brayshaw are away. They went on a cruise before Christmas."

Tears welled into her eyes when she heard who they were, and what their mission was.

"I heard it on the News. Whoever could have done such a thing?"

"You saw Miss Halliwell fairly frequently?"

"Well, not all that often, not in these last few years, since her grandfather became so ill and needed so much attention."

"But she used to do the laundry regularly for you?"

"Oh, yes, and so beautifully, too. And so much less roughly, you know, than these modern laundries."

"So she often came here with her basket?"

"Oh, no, scarcely ever recently. I used to miss her company, because she always stayed for a cup of tea in the kitchen. But Mrs. Brayshaw wouldn't let her make the journey—it was so much easier for her, you see, just to nip down to the village in the car."

"Yes, I'd heard that. But on this last occasion she came up with her cousin."

The housekeeper looked puzzled.

"Which last occasion was that, Sergeant?"

"Which newspaper do you take?" Wright asked.

"The *Telegraph*—but I haven't seen one for two weeks."

"In any case, it's the wrong one for what I had in mind. But Margaret came up here the day before she was killed."

"I'm sorry. I haven't set eyes on her since November."

It suddenly occurred to Wright that they had tripped up on an elementary question of timing. They had not established whether Calverley had crashed the car before or after delivering the washing. He turned to ask Russell if he knew the answer, but the constable was unable to help.

"But there wasn't any washing to be brought back," the housekeeper said, having followed the conversation with her eyes flitting from one face to the other. "It was all up to date. Margaret had nothing of ours. It had all come back, the week the Commander went away. When they're not at home, there's so little that I do it myself. I don't trouble Margaret."

"You're quite sure of this? There might not have been a few pairs of sheets that you'd overlooked?"

The housekeeper was still slightly bewildered.

"There couldn't have been. I keep a most careful inventory."

She would have liked, Wright could see, to participate in the inquest that was obviously going to be necessary. But he decided not to risk revealing any further information in her presence. And Wright's mind was racing round the problem that they had seen neither trace nor track of the car on the way up.

He did, however, discuss it openly with Russell as they buckled on their snow-shoes for the homeward track.

"This complicates the issue," he said.

"It certainly does, Sergeant."

"It might make a first-rate liar out of Calverley."

"I suppose it could."

"And it makes the newspaper cutting even more complex, and even more vital."

They came back to the edge of the precipice that overlooked the great expanse of ice.

"Just how intricate a problem is it going to be, if there never was a basket of linen?"

"I don't know," Russell said, and then, taking a deep breath, and exhaling noisily, "But there *was* a basket of linen. I saw it myself. And Kenworthy's not going to like this, but it's bound to come out sooner or later. *I* was responsible for that newspaper item. I saw them, you see, and I was feeling bloody sore."

"You must have worked damned fast."

"Too damned fast to think about the consequences, I suppose. There's a free-lance journalist down in Cotter Bridge that I know pretty well. Often have a pint with him. He covers this part of the world for one or two of the London papers—*when* anything happens. I told him about it."

"He'd be pleased!"

"I felt very satisfied with myself at the time. There's no doubt now where it's got me."

Wright thought of the cold white walk back to the Clough.

"Kenworthy's not going to like this," he repeated. "That's the understatement of the epoch. You've been a damned idiot, Russell."

And then he saw a shaft of hope.

"Still, you never know with Kenworthy. He works from his own book. You say you saw them with the basket?"

"Outside the Volunteer."

"And she got into his car?"

"After a bit of argument."

"And he drove her up this way?"

"No doubt about that."

"Well, find that bloody car for me, Russell. I can't promise you it will help, but it wouldn't do you any harm to get something right for a change."

◆ 12 ◆

KENWORTHY STOOD IN the shop doorway, smiling subtly, and watched his two assistants diminish into black dots against the white slopes.

"That'll larn 'em," he said, and Dick Haines, who judged that the remark was made to no one in particular, ventured no comment.

Kenworthy turned back into the village store, with its shelves of tinned foods, herbal packets, boiled sweets and bottles of Friar's Balsam glued to proprietary cards. There was a smell of dry-rot, candles, smoked bacon and carbolic soap.

"I suppose you get summer sightseers," he said. "In decent weather, the view from here must be worth a coach-trip."

"There's a few come up for the fishing. A few picnickers, Saturday afternoons and Sundays."

"I don't see any signs of catering for them."

"There's a few come in for a bottle of pop. I tried ice-cream one year, but there was no real demand for it."

"No farmhouse teas, or anything like that?"

"No. We don't do things on a very grand scale in Carrion Clough."

"These fishermen, then, what are they—day visitors?"

"They come up with cars and motor-bikes."

"You see what I'm getting at, don't you?"

Haines looked at him blankly. The shopkeeper was neither bright nor dull, neither disobliging nor anxious to help. From his age, he must have spent a few years in the army, but little of the world had rubbed off on him.

"If this job was the work of an outsider, it would be interesting to know who the regular visitors are."

He waited for Haines to volunteer firmly that it was not the work of an outsider, but Haines said nothing.

"Have you had any unusual customers in the shop in the last week or two? Any on *the* day?"

If any visitor wanted as little as a box of matches, he would have to go to Haines for it.

"None that I can think of," Haines said.

"You wouldn't have to think very hard."

"There's been none."

"The trouble with any crime," Kenworthy said, "is that only one person did it, but there's a stage in the inquiry when you suspect as many as forty."

He was beginning to find Haines tiresome.

"It's bound to cross my mind, for example, that you might have done it yourself."

This, at least, had some effect.

"Nay, Superintendent, steady on!"

"Your family lost land in the gathering grounds."

"Years ago. I was only a nipper. I didn't understand the talk there was about it."

"But you're not as well off now as you would have been if it hadn't happened."

"It makes no difference," Haines said. "I wouldn't have

gone on the land. Starve-acre, they called our farm. Bloody good name for it, too."

"Ben Drabble doesn't share your line of thought."

"Oh, Ben."

He looked more worried at the mention of Ben's name than he had been at being suspected himself. Perhaps he knew that Kenworthy was taking Ben a good deal more seriously.

"You don't want to take too much notice of the things Ben says. Ben broods."

"A dangerous thing to do," Kenworthy said.

"He's got damn all to brood about."

"He still feels out of pocket on those old deals. And they didn't call the Drabbles' farm Starve-acre."

"They'd have lost it anyway."

"They'd have got a better price from the Board than the Halliwells paid. Ben might not have been chipping ice for a living."

"No. He'd have been digging sheep out of drifts. Six of one—"

"It isn't the *reason* for it that counts," Kenworthy said. "This sort of thing only happens when reason looms too large. If you ask me, it isn't what the Halliwells did that rankles with Ben, it's the way they did it. They must have told some pretty poisonous lies about the prices the Board was prepared to pay."

"That was the way of it, certainly. But Ben—"

"Ben what?"

"Ben wouldn't do a thing like that. What would he have to gain from it?"

"What *did* anyone have to gain from it? Tell me that, my friend, what could anyone have gained from killing Margaret Halliwell?"

"The money."

"So all we've got to do is to spot someone trying to spend a few hundreds of antiquated Johnny Bradburies, and whip him in. That money could be nothing but an embarrassment to Chummy. And in any case, I find it difficult to believe that he robbed her of several hundred quid in a field in the dark in a snowstorm. Get me?"

Haines was not enjoying it. He did not want to be consulted. He did not like bringing his mind to bear on the crime. Kenworthy persevered.

"So let's say it wasn't the money. What does that leave us with? Either plain malice or perverted sentiment. Precisely the attitude of mind that your friend Ben has been expressing ever since I set eyes on him."

"I wish you'd leave Ben out of it. If you ask me, you don't have to look any further than them that lives up Moss Hill."

"And what makes you think that?"

"That's not for me to say."

"Why? Are you anti-social or something?"

"I don't know anything."

"Just supposition then, is it?"

"It stands out a mile," Haines said.

"I wish it did."

And at that moment a green bus arrived outside, and with it a small belated bundle of the day's newspapers.

"I'd like to know who has what," Kenworthy said. "Who takes the *Examiner*, for instance?"

"Only Mrs. Booth, and Ben."

"Thank you," Kenworthy said. "I'll be dropping in again some time."

He scanned the sky-line over above the reservoir, but was unable to locate Wright and Russell now. A huge crow flapped untidy wings from the bough of a sycamore, scattering powdery snow that fluttered for a moment in the air and then was gone.

Kenworthy made his way towards the Booths' cottage. It was time he made the acquaintance of Tommy's mother. When he had called before, he had made his way direct to the henhouse without coming across her. In fact he had taken every care to have Tommy to himself. But now it was Mrs. Booth he most wanted to see.

Kenworthy had imagined that she would be either an elderly slut, a timeless witch, or both, and first appearances confirmed the two images. A witch had to have an attendant animal, for that was the form in which her familiar attached himself to her, and as he crossed the threshold, Kenworthy tumbled over a lean and malicious cat that arched its back and spat defiance. A witch needed to have given a pinch of flesh in contract with her devil; and Mrs. Booth had a mole on the corner of her chin from which two white bristles grew obscenely. She was suffering from alopecia, and had a smooth bald patch under thin grey strands of hair, and she was wearing a drab woollen cardigan with an irregular, rough and badly matched darn covering most of one shoulder and the upper part of a sleeve.

But inside the cottage a certain cosy tidiness prevailed: a Silver Jubilee tea-caddy on the mantelpiece, and huge brown faded photographs of mutton-chopped ancestors on the walls. When she spoke, it was with venom and shrill anger at first, but before long Kenworthy was aware of an obvious foundation of discernment. He found he could omit stages of an argument, and she stayed with him.

"I hope you haven't come plaguing *him* again."

Tommy grinned happily at Kenworthy, whom he still regarded as his friend and potential conspirator in the matter of conveyancing the gathering grounds.

"Look at the poor loon! Anyone would think he was glad to see you."

"I haven't come to see Tommy."

"No? Well, if it's me you want to see, that'll cost you nothing. Tommy, go out and finish ridding in the back, there's a good boy."

Tommy lingered at the door. He wanted to see more of Kenworthy. But she drove him out with an angry cackle.

"Well?"

She had not asked Kenworthy to sit down. He helped himself to the only armchair.

"Just want to get to know you, that's all," he said.

"You've come fifty years too late."

"Tommy will have talked to you about the questions we asked him."

"Here we go."

"I'm not persecuting Tommy."

"Perhaps I'd better tell you from the start. I made him what he is. I tried to get rid of him. Pennyroyal. That's what's the matter with Tommy."

"I'm sorry for him, Mrs. Booth."

"Nice of you, I'm sure. I've no fancy ideas about Tommy. But no one wants to see their own flesh and blood on its way to Broadmoor."

"I don't think there's much danger of that, Mrs. Booth."

"So what's going to happen when he gets up in front of the court in Cotter Bridge? Did you *have* to do that to him? *She* gave him the box, and all the rubbish that was in it. *And* paid him off in solid gold. That's as good as a rope round his neck."

"We know all about that," Kenworthy said. "I think we accept that."

"What more do you want with him, then?"

"With *you*, I said. You take the *Examiner*, don't you?

You'll have read some of the bits about Calverley and Carrion Clough."

"I'm not interested."

"You must know a lot about the history of this village, Mrs. Booth. Tommy didn't get his knowledge—or his enthusiasm—from nowhere."

"I've talked to him."

"A lot. Because your own roots go pretty deep, don't they?"

"I'm seventy-five."

She went to a cupboard beside the fireplace, and brought out a heavily bound scrapbook.

"That's the history of Carrion Clough."

"Which Tommy knows by heart. I'd like to borrow that, Mrs. Booth."

She clutched it to her bosom and returned it to the cupboard, shaking her head. Kenworthy let it pass.

"Tommy used to work at Moss Hill Farm. They've given him the push now, I suppose."

"That's Edith for you."

"You don't care for the Halliwells?"

"Pigs can only grunt."

"I suppose you're another of those who still carry ill-feeling for the land negotiations."

She laughed emptily.

"My father had no land."

"But you're a native?"

"A native? Aye. Bone through my nose and all."

"And who do you think killed Margaret Halliwell?"

"How should I know?"

"You must have wondered yourself whether it might have been Tommy."

"You know it wasn't."

"Why so sure?"

"You know very well where he was when the gun went off."

"And where were you?"

"In here."

"Alone?"

"After me now, are you? Margaret's the only one of that brood I wouldn't shoot, if I had the chance."

"Why?"

"Because Margaret was a—"

"I mean the others."

She looked as if she were going to spit into the fire, but instead shaped the embers slowly and neatly with a poker.

"You wouldn't believe me if I told you. And if you did, you'd probably arrest me."

Perhaps she was being enigmatic for the fun of it. Again, he decided not to press her.

"I'd like to see Tommy again," he said, "only this time, I'd like you with me. You can probably keep him on the rails for me. His mind has a tendency to wander when I talk to him."

She went through a scullery and called him from behind the cottage.

"Mr. Kenworthy wants to ask you some questions. Speak up and don't talk twaddle."

Tommy beamed, and sat down on a kitchen chair with his cap on.

"I want to know exactly when it was that Miss Margaret paid you your wages, Tommy, all that gold."

"The morning after her grand-dad died," Tommy said simply.

"And where did she get it from?"

"From her grand-dad."

Sweetness and patience.

"I mean, where in the room did she get it from? From a drawer, a cupboard, a box?"

"It was on the table."

"Did she give you all the money that was on the table? Or was there a lot more?"

"She'd counted it out for me. It was my wages."

"It was a bonus," his mother said. "*And* he'd earned it. And it's no use asking him where she'd hid the rest of it. There's a lot of people in the Clough *and* up Moss Hill who'd like to know that. I would, for one—I'm a shareholder, too."

"You've worked at the farm too, in your time, have you?"

"Like hell!"

He concentrated on Tommy.

"How long had you been in the hen-house, when Constable Russell came and found you?"

Tommy looked dim. Kenworthy looked at his mother for assistance.

"Not long," she said. "That was the afternoon Edith sacked him. Because he'd gone into the kitchen without knocking to get hot water for the pump. That's how he came to be home early."

"And on your way back, you went up to the tree, didn't you?"

"No," Tommy said.

"To get the gun."

"No."

"But you knew the gun was there."

Tommy was silent. There was enough guile in him for him to know that a truthful answer might incriminate him. His mother looked on placidly, but with a beady intelligence in her eyes.

"And the money, that was in the tree too, wasn't it?"

"No," he answered. "She never put the money there."

"You know? You'd looked?"

"I'd told him to," Mrs. Booth said. "I'd not have been ashamed to take my due."

"What due was that?"

"For services rendered."

"You'd mixed the old man a spell at some time or other, had you?" Kenworthy risked.

"You can call it that if you like."

"That afternoon, Tommy, you got home early. How long did you stay in here before you went to the hen-house?"

"Dunno."

"Not long, Mr. Kenworthy."

"It seems odd, doesn't it, to have gone out in the gathering dark to look at his papers?"

"He took the hurricane lamp. Wasting oil on that rubbish."

"And the shot was how long after that?"

"A few minutes. Say a quarter of an hour."

"Did *you* know that P.C. Russell had gone to the hen-house?"

"No. And he'd no right—"

"Tommy, on your way down from the farm, after Edith had given you the sack, did you see anybody coming up?"

"Only Mr. Shelmerdine," Tommy said.

"Mr. Shelmerdine?"

But his mother was suddenly very angry.

"Tommy! You're talking silly, now. He gets things mixed up, Mr. Kenworthy."

"Who's Mr. Shelmerdine?"

"He died fifty years ago."

"Did he say anything to you, Tommy?"

Mrs. Booth was ready to blaze.

"How could he?"

"I'm asking Tommy."

Tommy shook his head. He dared not say anything in front of his mother.

"This Mr. Shelmerdine, Mrs. Booth? Who was he? What was he like?"

"Silly talk," she said.

But she was rattled. Kenworthy knew that she had come to the same conclusion as he had, but had gone a stage further than him because of her local knowledge. Kenworthy now knew that someone had arrived at Moss Hill Farm at approximately the time when Margaret was leaving the house in a huff. And like himself, Mrs. Booth had found this out within the last few seconds. But there was this difference: Mrs. Booth knew who it was. There was a smoke of smouldering thought in her eyes.

"This Mr. Shelmerdine . . ." Kenworthy's tone changed. Only to a certain point could he cajole the old hag. Now he had to risk driving her to antagonism. "Who was he?"

She hesitated to refuse to answer, then shrugged her shoulders.

"He was Secretary to the Water Board, at the time when they were building the dam."

"Have you a picture of him in one of your albums?"

Again she seemed on the point of stubborn refusal. But after a pause she hobbled over to the cupboard. Tommy craned forward eagerly at the sight of the scrapbook. He loved it. The pair of them must have pored over it hour after hour by lamplight on winter evenings, glorying in the past.

Mrs. Booth turned the pages. They were mostly newspaper cuttings, yellow, foxed and curling at the edges. The paste was lumpy under the newsprint. Tommy got up and bent over his mother's shoulder. She pushed him away almost savagely with her elbow, putting the book down where only she and Kenworthy could see it.

"Here we are. This was the group when the dam was opened."

They were pompous men with chains of office, foundation stones and gavels.

"Who are all these people?"

"Oh, I don't know them all. They'd a lot of big-wigs from the cities that were going to get the water. Look: there's Thomas John and his father, you can just see their faces."

Moustached, self-conscious, serious-minded, not in the platform party, lost in the second tier of the crowd.

"That's old man Drabble. Caleb Wardle. Horncastle, the solicitor. That's Isaac Pennington's grandfather. Old Samuel Haines—and this is Mr. Shelmerdine."

Tall, lean, distinguished, a long, sad face, with high cheekbones and drooping whiskers, on the front row of the platform, senior official, to the left of the fat-gutted democrats.

Kenworthy gazed at the picture.

So they were looking for a man of six foot three, straight as a ram-rod, fleshless, high forehead, aquiline nose, thin lipped, long limbed. Beyond that they need not go. In matching similarities, Tommy Booth was no purist.

But a tall man, six foot three, lean, long limbed. So far, no such figure had appeared on the scene at Carrion Clough.

• 13 •

WRIGHT AND RUSSELL made their flat-footed way back along the track that edged the precipitous quarries.

"At any rate, he didn't come off the road on this stretch," Wright said. "If they'd tumbled down that lot, we'd have heard a different kind of story."

And on the opposite side the hillside rose at an angle of eighty degrees, with not a yard to spare at the edge of the track.

"That cuts out the whole of this stretch. What beats me is that we didn't see a trace of it on the way up. You can't *lose* an Austin Princess."

"You can lose anything in a fifteen-foot drift," Russell said. "They lost a bus in Cotter Bridge, the winter after I came out of the army. In the cattle market, it was. Three weeks it was missing."

They looked across the reservoir to the few huddled cottages that remained of Carrion Clough. On the hillside beyond, a wisp of smoke hung above the roof of Moss Hill Farm. Russell stood for a moment with his jaw muscles visibly tensed. Wright guessed what turn his thoughts had taken.

"Come on," he said abruptly. "We've got to bloody well find it, and we shan't do it admiring the scenery."

They plodded on.

"I'm thinking," Russell said. "All the way up from the dam the road climbs between those tight banks. Till it comes to the intersection with this track. That's the only place they could have gone astray. Anywhere else, they'd have blocked the road."

"Let's get there, then."

The wind was in their faces now, a spiteful, unremitting blast from the north-east that had behind it all the malice of ice-locked northern Europe. It was a thin, penetrating shaft, against which a man could almost lean, and it found inexorably the square half-inch where one's muffler was badly crossed about one's throat. By common consent they stopped after ten minutes and turned their backs to it. Wright got out a cigarette, and had to make a tent of his coat to get a light to it.

"You work a lot with Kenworthy?" Russell asked.

It was only Wright's second major case with the superintendent, but he saw no point in underlining his inexperience.

"He seems to have got into the habit of asking for me," he said.

"What sort of chap is he?"

Wright did his best at a cynical chuckle.

"Short of writing a book about him. . . ."

"I mean, I'm damned if I know what to make of him."

"That's a common complaint. I don't think he always knows what to make of himself."

"He didn't make his reputation on indecision, though, did he?"

"No. He made it on sheer inscruta-bloody-bility. He has 'em all fooled. That's how he does it."

"He has me fooled all right."

"He *will* have you fooled."

"You mean when you tell him about that bit in the newspaper?"

"It would pay you to tell him yourself. I'll make the opening for it, if it'll make it easier for you."

"How's he going to take it?"

Wright laughed, not kindly. He saw no great reason for kid-gloving Russell at this stage.

"It depends on how much of this morning he's already spent on this gossip column."

"He'll have my guts."

"Go on thinking that, and you won't be disappointed. But don't give up hope. He's let you off once. He must like you."

Russell thought.

"It's crossed my mind more than once that he only let me off the hook because he still thinks I'm the one he's after. I'm right, aren't I?"

"Ask yourself."

"I can't blame him for thinking it, I suppose. My only alibi depends upon my own word—and Tommy Booth's. Fat lot of good that might do me."

"What put you on to Tommy Booth, anyway?"

"I saw him go into the hen-house. He seemed to be spending a long time there. Lucky guess. Doesn't help, does it?"

He looked again over to Moss Hill.

"If only I could get the bastard . . ."

A fresh face, young for his years. He had got up this morning sure that this was going to be the day of his life. And there was enough romance left in him for him to

picture himself pulling off a coup where two Scotland Yard
men had failed. And it might well need something of about
that calibre to save him.

"If we go back and tell Kenworthy we couldn't find that
car," Wright said, "we shall both be for the dufter."

They braved the wind again. Every step was hard work.
Wright resisted the temptation to stop again, pushing one
foot in front of the other until he reached a state in which
each new pace demanded a conscious effort. Russell kept up
with him without speaking again. At last they reached the
intersection of ways, where a right-angled turn would take
them down the road up which they had come.

The spot was a kind of clearing at the head of a valley, the
snow uneven, but its humps and ridges probably bearing no
relationship to the contours that lay beneath.

"It must be under here somewhere," Russell said.

"Digging at random could take us the best part of a week.
We'd better make a start. I assume he went off course at the
point where he made the left turn. Does that make sense,
from your knowledge of the ground?"

Russell furrowed his brow.

"It doesn't seem likely. He'd have to skirt a bit of a
hollow—about there, see?—but I wouldn't have thought
he'd have foundered in it."

He brought out the two pieces of his entrenching tool and
assembled it, going to work at once. After a few minutes, he
threw off his raincoat and later even his jacket, flailing away
with the inadequate instrument so that snow flew up in a
continuous fountain. Presently he had dug a trench down to
ground level for a length about twelve feet, and began to
drive off radial arms from it. When he stopped for breath,
beads of sweat running incongruously down his face,
Wright took the tool from his hands and doubled to himself.
But at the end of half an hour there was nothing to show for

their labours except dead damp grass and boulders of millstone grit.

"I'm tempted to wait for the thaw," Wright said.

"What's so important about the car, anyway? It's not going to solve the murder for us, is it?"

"Kenworthy said find the car. I'm afraid that means find it.

Russell stood back and surveyed his handiwork in dismay and perplexity.

"Well, it's not in *this* hollow."

He looked wild-eyed round the spacious clearing.

"And digging at random's an insane way of tackling it."

He walked away from the trenches they had dug and looked over the brow where their earlier footprints were already crisply frozen in the cart-track from the dam.

"Obviously he came up here. And obviously he didn't turn and slew into this hollow. That means he missed the left turn. Understandable enough, because visibility must have been down to nil. Therefore he must have ploughed on, the ground getting bumpier and bumpier as he went."

He began to dig again, throwing snow into the air with a violence little short of frenzy, and following the line of the continuation of the track.

"Of course, as soon as he realized he was off his course— and Margaret would have seen it before he did—he might have tried to reverse out of it, and probably half heeled over. I don't think he'd have got very far. This might not take us too long."

"Wright went to his help with his hands, throwing the snow up between his legs, like a dog burying a bone. Their earlier effort had seemed a massive task, but the job they had now set themselves was Herculean.

After half an hour, they rested. Wright felt as if perspiration had soaked through every layer of garment he was wearing. And the keenness of the wind was unabated.

"I've often wondered whether I should die on duty. But that meant revolver shots on London roof-tops. I never thought of Arctic exploration."

"If we have to stop overnight, we might try making an igloo about mid-afternoon," Russell suggested.

They had made considerable inroads into the snow, and the narrow channels they had carved gave the scene an even greater air of grotesque abandon than it had had previously. There was soft brown slush where their feet had stamped down to ground level.

"We need proper shovels."

"If we go off to fetch tackle, we shall be beaten by daylight. I wish we'd brought something to eat."

"I'd willingly flog my kayak for a handful of blubber."

Back to work. Twice they made trial diggings to left and right of their main working, and were never certain how long to persevere before they returned to their central axis.

Then Russell stooped and picked something up. It was a man's string-backed driving glove.

"Success! They've been here!"

The certainty of it had begun to recede. Now they were so excited that they began to thrash at the snow like demented creatures.

"He may have stopped here to try to clear his windscreen."

Stooping, Russell chopped into a drift with the edge of his implement, and suddenly met resistance. With his fingertips, he scraped his way down to a hub-cap. Wright rushed to his side.

But even when they knew where the vehicle was, it was a heart-breaking effort getting down to the shape of it.

"Careful of his paint-work!"

"Bugger his paint-work!"

All their accumulated frustration and the sudden energy of requitement were canalized into a bout of hatred of Calverley. Wright wiped snow from a doorhandle and tried it.

"Trust him to have locked it!"

"Do our Crime Prevention Officer's heart good, that would!"

Russell went to the pocket of his raincoat and brought out a selection of a couple of dozen keys on a twist of wire.

"We might be lucky. It's a good job we have a parking problem in Cotter Bridge."

They had to strike a series of matches to thaw the ice out of the keyhole. And then Russell tried to insert one key after another, finally giving one a twist with a crow of jubilation. He tugged hard at the door, broke the crackling ice of its crevices with the sheer ebullient strength of elation. And at once the silence of the moors was assailed by an ear-splitting klaxon.

"My God! The daft bugger's left his burglar-alarm on."

In Pimlico or Parliament Square, it would have brought a squad car at the double. In this frozen desolation it aroused no more than the screech of a jackdaw in one of the old quarries. And somewhere a sheep bleated, to be answered by several cousins in remote hollows. It was harmless— only two men in the whole of creation could hear it—but it was unnerving: a loud, high-pitched, insistent scream, that made conversation impossible.

"For God's sake try to stop it!"

Russell felt with his fingers around the inside of the door frame, lighted on the spigot of a switch, and for a blessed moment there was silence. Then he took his hand away, and the thing started again.

Wright was suddenly unreasonably angry with Russell.

"Don't mess about! Find some way of stopping it!"

"Sorry, Sarge. We'll have to find some way of holding this thing down."

He turned round, creating temporary peace again, and grinned to show that he took no offence at Wright's outburst.

"Look, Sarge. You hold the switch down, and I'll try to clear the bonnet. Though without a wiring diagram, I may not know where to start. There are so many different makes of these damned things."

"I can see why a car-thief might panic!"

It took Russell minutes to have the lid of the bonnet up, and then, seconds later, with a triumphant tug, he snatched away the bare ends of two wires.

"O.K., Sarge."

Wright opened the door and climbed into the front passenger seat. A warm, familiar and slightly stale smell of upholstery. He opened the door of the glove-pocket: maps, an R.A.C. Year Book, a London A to Z, a few House of Commons Order Papers, looking oddly like an exhibit from an alien world, with local authorities' private bills preceding the afternoon's business. It was as if Calverley had to strew reminders of his professional success about him wherever he went.

And there was a small hip-flask half full of whisky.

Wright shifted over to the driver's seat and called Russell.

"Come and have a shot of Stag's Breath, Jim. Get a spot of warmth into your veins."

They passed the flask from one to the other, and sat for a while recuperating: strong men exhausted, but they rapidly revived.

"We've made it. And how much forrader are we? I can see damn all for our pains."

Wright leaned over the back of the seat, clawing the safety belt out of his way, and examined the capacious rear-seat. With difficulty he stretched down his arm and picked up from the floor a hair-grip, which he forbore to mention to Russell. Otherwise there was nothing.

"You're sure they had the linen-basket with them?"

"Positive."

"And you saw them lift it into the back seat?"

"Dead sure."

"Well, they must have transferred it to the boot. Come, lad, buckets and spades to the fore again."

There was five feet of snow over the back of the car. So near and yet so far, the new outburst of labour was agonizing. And all to do again with frozen lock and car key.

But at last they had the lid up, and the basket was there, unevenly balanced on the jack, looking strangely clean and clinical with a smoothly ironed huckaback towel stretched over its contents.

"That housekeeper must have made a mistake over her inventory."

Wright lifted a corner of the towel and saw, not a pile of laundered linen, but layer after layer of bundled bank-notes: green, blue, green, blue: of every shade and vintage. And there was a pile of at least twenty small brown bags of the kind in which banks give small change. He opened one and pulled out a half-sovereign.

"Well, the smooth bloody operator!"

And then tucking the towel back into position, "You know, I'm damned certain Calverley never knew this lot was here. Even after all that happened, I think Margaret would have kept her own counsel about this. A smart lass. What a bloody wonderful way of getting it into safe keeping! Well, Jim, I've got an idea Kenworthy may forgive you, after all. I'll let him know this was mostly your work. Now we've got to get this lot back to the village. It's going to be a damned awkward walk."

They lifted out the basket and set it down on the snow, closed the boot, helped themselves to the remaining drops of whisky, locked the car doors and took one last look about them before beginning the descent.

"Prehistoric, that's what it is," Wright said. "Who'd have thought that that thing was careering up the M.I less than a fortnight ago?"

They each took a handle of the basket and started down the steep track. And as there were places in which they could not walk abreast, progress seemed even slower than the way up had been.

"Hell, it's heavy!" Wright said. "She'd never have got it up here on her own."

"You didn't know Margaret Halliwell. When she'd got an idea into her head."

Wright looked at his wrist-watch: a quarter to three.

"Break for a smoke!"

They put the basket on the flat top of a wall. Russell did not smoke. He beat circulation back into his numbed left hand whilst Wright cursed the flame of his lighter.

"I shan't be sorry to get back to an honest round of metropolitan pickpockets."

Then, stepping up to grasp the basket again, the rim of his snow-shoe twisted over against a concealed tuft of bracken. He lunged sideways and caught the basket with his shoulder. Russell rushed to the rescue, but too late. They clambered up to the wall in time to see the furrow that the basket had ploughed down the long frozen slope. And then they saw it heel over the edge of one of the sheer drops, turning on its side and scattering bundles of notes into the snow.

Russell vaulted the wall, righted himself at the other side.

"Careful, now. You'll break your neck down there."

But Russell came as near to running down the slope as his awkward foot-gear would allow him. He stopped to pick up one wad of notes which had fallen out on this side of the precipice. But he went no further.

When he got back to the wall, he was in deep dudgeon.

"It's fallen ninety feet. Vertical drop. Money all over the bloody auction. There's no way down in these conditions. Our only hope is to make our way up. And that means crossing the reservoir on the ice. I'll do it."

"Not enough daylight left today. And it would be suicide after dark. Mind you, Kenworthy'll kill us—*me*, I mean."

·14·

KENWORTHY WALKED UP from the Booth's cottage, quickening his steps when he saw Judson's car outside the Volunteer.

"A lot of stuff in for you, Superintendent. Reports on all those things you sent to London for."

The county inspector handed over a buff file. Kenworthy glanced cursorily at the top sheet.

"More dope about Calverley. By and large I could write a case-book on him by now. Very interesting. And utterly futile. Got a mug-book on you?"

"In the car."

"Would you mind getting it? I'll show you the man we're after."

Kenworthy juggled with the transparent sheets of the Identikit and finally produced a likeness of Shelmerdine.

"I was a fat-head not to bring her scrapbook with me. But we're not dealing with close similarity. Roughly speaking a tall man, six foot three, ram-rod straight, distinguished looking and on the melancholy side. Mean anything to you?"

"Nothing. I'll swear there have been no strangers in the village."

"I'm satisfied someone was going up to the farm as Tommy Booth was coming away."

He put Judson briefly into the picture.

"Changes the situation," Judson said. "And doesn't surprise me. It's the only logical solution, come to think about it. But he got away unseen—except by Tommy. And you can bet your bull's-eye he won't be back."

"They sometimes turn up at the funeral," Kenworthy said wistfully, "and that's this afternoon. What did you make of Tommy's mother?"

"Bloody old witch."

"I'll grant you they'd have ducked her in cow-piss a couple of centuries ago. But they were pretty liberal with that commodity for anyone they didn't understand."

"Half crazed old bag."

"Plus."

Judson looked at him keenly.

"Not without brains," Kenworthy said. "Gave me a run for my money. And she knows the identity of this man we're calling Shelmerdine. But boiling oil wouldn't get it out of her at this juncture. And I'm interested in her background. There's something about her attitude to the old village that puts her in a class apart. And her weird line of talk of the debt the Halliwells owed her—which had nothing to do with land-grabbing. Known better days, perhaps? Was there ever a Mr. Booth? Have you come across anything?"

"I didn't think it worth while going into detail. There was a husband. He walked out on her in the nineteen twenties. Can't say I blame him. Never heard of since. That's the Clough story. I dare say we could dig deeper."

"I think we shall have to," Kenworthy said. "Just in case

he was a tall man with a sad face. God knows, he'd have reason enough for that."

He settled down to read the typescript case reports, which he eventually laid aside with a sigh.

"As I thought, doesn't help us much. Calverley has a patron. That doesn't surprise me. Nothing wrong in it, intrinsically. Commandant of his O.C.T.U. Spotted talent, no doubt. No suggestion of homosexuality. Thank God; I never did care for it. Had Calverley transferred to his own staff when they gave him a brigade of his own. From there to brigade major in short, easy stages. I don't mind. A brigadier's entitled to a staff officer he feels he can trust. But then Brig turns up as chairman of a constituency parliamentary party after the war. Calverley's constituency. Again, fair enough. Brig plays safe and brings a man after his own heart to the hustings. I'd like to meet this brigadier, all the same, though I don't think it would do us any good."

"Stands about six foot three, I suppose, with a spine like a poker."

Kenworthy put the flat of his hands on the table.

"See how it goes? Find a motive, couldn't we, with a touch of imagination? Jealous of protégé. Sees brilliant young prospects ruined by injudicious affair. Drag in the homo element by the scruff of its neck, if we felt like it. Gets under the counter tip from the *Examiner* offices and hares up here to sort things out. Bloody ridiculous! Timing's hopelessly wrong. Watch it, Inspector. You're in danger of your own zeal. I wonder what our two lads are up to? Got so little for them to do today that I sent them out for a country walk. Some people would spend a fortune to go buggering about in the snow."

There was enough of the morning left for Kenworthy to pursue some of his more recent thoughts, and he took Judson with him to call on Wilfred Wilson.

Wilson received them this time, not in the schoolroom, but in his own study, a drab, infrequently heated upstairs room, lined with an uninspiring collection of books, and with armchairs, carpeting and various unmatched articles of furniture that had obviously been relegated there at the end of their effective life in the rooms over which his wife exercised some taste.

The schoolmaster was dressed in black, all ready for the funeral bar collar and tie, and there was something uncharacteristically remote and unhappy in his bearing that showed even in a thoughtful slowness of speech. He was surprisingly unpleased to see them, and even his attempts at good humour were superficial and unconvincing.

"They've asked me to act as a bearer. That's a bit of Edith for you—living it up, in her fashion. Well, this afternoon old Thomas John's going to put us to the test. We shall see for ourselves whether he'll let us bury him nor not."

Then silence: the old joke pressed too far. Wilson waited for the superintendent to begin. And Kenworthy's hands were cold. He was wondering what Wilson had on his mind.

"I really wanted to ask you whether the name Shelmerdine means anything to you."

Wilson was either genuinely puzzled, or else his thoughts were far away. He scarcely seemed to have heard the question.

"Shelmerdine," Kenworthy repeated.

"No. The name doesn't ring a bell."

Silence again. Wilson was incurious. He did not even seem to want to know.

"He was Secretary of the Water Board at the time of the take-over," Kenworthy prompted.

"Well. God, that's ancient history. Twenty years before *I* came to Carrion Clough. That's a long time, gentlemen."

Again Wilson relapsed into comparative vacancy.

"But you hear all the gossip there is in the village, Mr. Wilson. You've heard all the folk-lore a hundred times over. The Secretary of the Board——"

"I've never heard the name mentioned. I'd have remembered if I had. It's an unusual name."

The three men looked at each other, then Wilson volunteered an explanation, as if by mighty effort.

"Secretary of the Board, you know, he'd be a city man. Wouldn't have had much contact with the village. And three generations ago."

What was Wilson uneasy about? What did he know? Kenworthy considered; and decided to risk displaying his cards.

"Well, I may be stirring up a mare's nest at that. After all, this is only another case of mistaken identity by Tommy Booth."

Wilson smiled thinly.

"A tall, slender man, upright, distinctive, unhappy looking, whom Tommy Booth, thinking of an old picture, mistook for this Mr. Shelmerdine. Does that get us anywhere?"

"There's no one in Carrion Clough that fits that description."

Wilson himself was neither tall nor slender. Unhappy-looking certainly, but there was no likelihood that Tommy Booth would ever mistake him for anyone else, in any light or at any reasonable distance.

"I know you've got to follow up every lead you can get, gentlemen, but you don't need me to tell you not to attach too much weight to anything you get from Tommy."

"There's no smoke without fire," Kenworthy said.

"I've yet to see Tommy burst into flames."

"What can you tell me about Mrs. Booth?" Kenworthy asked suddenly.

"A half crazed old harridan."

"Was she always like that?"

"People say she's known better days."

"What was her relationship with the Halliwells?"

Wilson thought about this, but in some bewilderment.

"It's news to me that there ever was one."

"If there had have been, people would have talked, wouldn't they?"

"I've never heard anything."

"There was a Mr. Booth at one period. He deserted her, I understand."

"That was round about the time when I actually moved in here," Wilson said. "Of course, it was a nine-day wonder. But that's forty years ago."

"Did you know her husband?"

"I remember seeing him."

"What sort of man was he?"

"He was a cut above Carrion Clough, from what I heard tell. Not a local man, though he settled here after he married her. He'd travelled a bit, I think, done more than one type of job. Just what work he did in Carrion Clough I don't think I ever really knew."

"Why did he leave her?"

"Why did he ever saddle himself with her in the first instance, you mean?"

"Well, why did he? Obviously she's deteriorated. Obviously forty years as a derelict, with no better company than Tommy, have not left her entirely the woman she was."

"I think that's true. But I can't tell you much. She was always insular. And the village has always hated her."

"Like a witch."

"Precisely. They hate her now simply because she's as wretched as she is. They hated her in the old days because she fancied herself. At least, so I've heard."

It seemed as if Wilson were over some sort of obstacle. He was beginning to get into conversational stride.

"And on what grounds did she fancy herself?"

"How do I know? Her family didn't amount to anything. Her father was the village cobbler, and she'd been out for a few years in town in service. That was about all there was for a girl in those days. I don't know when she came back home, or why. And I don't think there's anyone left who could tell you. She was undoubtedly a better looker than she is today. And she might have picked up some big ideas from some of the houses in which she worked."

"She's no fool," Kenworthy said tentatively.

"It depends what you mean by a fool. She hasn't exactly invested her talents, has she?"

"I mean, she struck me as having a fairly sharp brain."

"But thoroughly mixed up."

"The two go together, often enough. And she certainly has an obsession with the past. That's where Tommy gets all his muddled history from."

"That's true," Wilson said, "but it's not in itself sinister, is it? I'm going to have an obsession with the past the moment I leave here. There'll be damn all else to live for."

This was unadulterated bitterness. Perhaps there was nothing wrong with the man except the end of his own epoch.

"Superintendent, far be it from me to try to teach you your job. And I'm sure you find these bygones fascinating. But you're delving pretty deep. Do you really think that anything in Ada Booth's past has any connection with who shot Margaret Halliwell?"

Kenworthy looked covertly at Judson, who had not spoken a word since they came into the room. He felt fairly certain that the county inspector, too, thought he was wasting his time.

"I've held all along," he said, "that the answer to all this lies under the water."

He rose to go, and Judson lumbered to his feet.

"You'll be at the funeral, I suppose," Wilson said.

"I wouldn't miss it for a small fortune."

"See you tonight in the Volunteer, perhaps."

✦ 15 ✦

THEY WAITED IN Judson's car until the funeral cortège came down the steep lane from Moss Hill Farm; two hearses, three black taxis, a quarter of an hour later than expected, as if things had been going wrong from the start, which was not surprising, in view of the difficulty of manœuvring the enormous shining cars in the snow.

Kenworthy looked closely at the occupants of the vehicles as they passed. There were no strangers, other than the augmented undertaker's team, and none of those, at a quick glance, who bore any resemblance to the legendary Shelmerdine. Though Edith Calverley was ram-rod straight, and no doubt considered her appearance distinguished. And Anthony was staring glassily, deliberately not seeing the police car. In the last taxi were the men from the village: Ben Drabble, Dick Haines, Isaac Pennington, and Wilfred Wilson sitting in front beside the driver.

It was a drive of some five or six miles. After the readjustment of parishes, following the flooding of the valley, Carrion Clough had buried its dead in a little churchyard on a hillside at the south-west corner of the water almost overlooking Warburton Hall, but separated from it by the wide, frozen chasm of the reservoir. A huge, wedge-shaped wooden plough had gone out that morning, drawn by four horses, to ensure a passage for the procession.

"Well," Kenworthy said, "this is going to take a weight off the Clough. I think Ben Drabble will begin to feel a bit better when Thomas John's been planted. The Clough can return to normal, then."

"Normal?" Judson said. "Aye, that's a thought."

"The village doesn't exactly scintillate with a future, does it?"

"Is there any particular reason why it should have a future? This isn't London, Superintendent."

They were climbing up a hairpin bend in bottom gear. Huge stalagmatic waves of ice clasped the tumbled boulders of a steep mountain brook. Judson braked suddenly to avoid a pair of sheep, eyeing them furtively from the side of the road, who decided at the crucial moment to make a frantic dash in front of the car.

"No. It isn't London," Kenworthy said. "I keep having to remind myself that even this ride is part of our working process. I don't know what we're likely to find out this afternoon."

Judson said nothing. There was more and more suggestion of silent accusation in his attitude to his specialist colleague.

"I was tempted to add Wilfred Wilson to my list of suspects at one stage this morning."

"Got to suspect everybody," Judson said listlessly.

"I can't see why, though. Can't find the faintest semblance of a motive for him. I think he was just preoccupied with his own future."

"He's reason enough for that. Spent all his money on ale,

and no better prospects than a council house in Cotter Bridge. If he can get one."

The road ceased to climb, and they drove at rather more than conventional funeral speed along a narrow level lane. The windows were quickly steamed up, and Kenworthy worked constantly with a duster to keep them clear.

"Well, Wilson might want the money," he said. "It might be worth digging around to see if he had any sense that the Halliwells were in his debt."

"I think you're scraping the bottom of the barrel, there, Superintendent."

"I'm bloody sure I am. I don't mind admitting I'm lost. And I'd be a good deal happier if I could think of something positive to do. Now what's up?"

They had stopped, close up behind the car in front. Minutes passed. Judson switched off the engine, and the car grew cold. Presently, the undertaker came and tapped on the window.

"Sorry about the delay, gentlemen. We've caught up with the plough. One of the horses has fallen and broken a leg. They've sent for a vet from Cotter Bridge to come and shoot it."

"By God, I'd like to see Ben Drabble's face now," Kenworthy said.

Half an hour later, Judson had to back on to an almost impossibly narrow verge to let a little white utility van pass. Shortly afterwards there was a single, brittle, resonant shot. A plover went wheeling and screeching into the air above them.

"All done by Thomas John," Kenworthy said.

They drove past the carcase, moved slowly now that they were in the immediate wake of the depleted plough. When they reached the gate of the churchyard, Kenworthy wound down the window, in spite of the cold. He scanned the faces of the group standing by the lych-gate: the vicar, with his stole streaming in the wind, Calverley and his mother, the Pollards, Wilson and the other local men, Horncastle, the solicitor, and a number of young men, some of them tall and straight, probably newspaper reporters.

I am the Resurrection and the Life . . .

It was a bleak, exposed spot, on the open corner of a hillside. The malevolent wind that had whipped Wright and Russell was no less merciful to their less athletic elders. Faces were pinched up and noses blue. The two detectives padded discreetly behind the last of the mourners, led by Edith on Anthony's arm, his eyes glazed.

Snow was still drifting. A flurry was whipped up on the edge of a dune. A way had been dug along the main pathway, but the sexton had had all he could do to prepare two graves in the solid, frozen earth. They came to a spot where the bearers were up to their knees in snow and had to stop, working in pairs in an endless chain, passing the coffin over their heads.

Then Wilson suddenly screamed, not hysterically, rather a loud groan, and fell away from the coffin with his hand on his heart. The man behind him stumbled over him, then went to his rescue. The cruel edges of the coffin slipped from numbed fingers in the confusion. The yellow box behaved as if it had been thrown through the air, landing sideways on the top of a low yew hedge. For a moment it slithered, then toppled over the other side.

Kenworthy and Judson rushed to look. There was a steep incline. The coffin had hit solid ice and slid fifty feet to come to rest with its end in a drift.

Other men were looking.

"We shall need a crane."

"There's no way of getting at him till the thaw comes."

A press photographer had leaped into eager action. Others were doing their best for Wilson.

"Don't worry about me," the schoolmaster said. "It's passed. I've had it off and on these last few days. I'm all right now. *Anno domini,* that's all it is."

Kenworthy looked round for Ben Drabble. The waterman was standing apart from the others, trembling visibly.

• 16 •

BY A LITTLE skilful jockeying, Kenworthy managed to have Wilson transported to hospital in Horncastle's chauffeur-driven car. And Wilson, feebly and vainly protesting that his own bed for a few days was all he needed, was driven down to Cotter Bridge with Isaac Pennington for company.

This gave Kenworthy the opportunity to ferry Horncastle home in Judson's car. And immediately after the interment of Margaret, which was dispatched with as much speed as was consonant with reasonable decency, the ageing solicitor was ensconced in a corner of the back seat.

The old man, well muffled as he was—almost lost indeed in the folds of his fur-collared greatcoat—had stood up to the elements with fewer signs of distress than many of his juniors. There was an air of distinction about the long white hair that curled from under his black Homburg, and the essence of a forgotten era seemed to emanate from his very presence.

Sitting in the further corner, leaving respectful space between them, Kenworthy turned down towards him and looked him full in the face.

"Shelmerdine! What can you tell me about Shelmerdine?"

The old man's aplomb was rooted in years of cultured aloofness, but he moistened his lower lip with the tip of his tongue. Kenworthy had intended the surname to take the solicitor by surprise, but could not be sure how well he had succeeded.

"Shelmerdine? What do you know of Shelmerdine?"

"Nothing. That's why I'm asking you, sir."

"You must have been digging pretty deep into local history if you have unearthed a reference to Shelmerdine. I can't see how it can possibly help you in your researches."

"I've become interested in all kinds of side-lines. What can you tell me about him?"

"He was Secretary of the Board. An engineer. Trained at Owen's College. The whole idea of flooding Carrion Clough was his brain-child. He died, oh, let me see, before the First World War."

"Did he leave any dependants?"

"I really could not say. He did not belong to Carrion Clough—or even Cotter Bridge. But why this close interest in Shelmerdine?"

Horncastle moved in his seat sufficiently to unbutton his greatcoat and bring out a handsomely engraved silver snuffbox, which he offered to Kenworthy. Kenworthy gravely accepted, and took a pinch from the back of his thumb. Judson slowed to pass the spot at which the plough-horse had been slaughtered.

Kenworthy changed the subject.

"I presume you know Thomas Booth?"

"By repute."

"I suppose you also know of Booth's mother?"

"Again, by repute. Superintendent, my contact with Carrion Clough these days is exiguous. For the last thirty years, Thomas John Halliwell was my last remaining client in the valley."

"What was her repute?" Kenworthy persisted.

"Oh! This is ancient gossip, Superintendent."

"I am interested in ancient gossip. I can find nothing in the nineteen sixties to justify this brutal killing."

"But I do not know how Mrs. Booth can help you. She was, oh, not even a harlot. An aspiring amateur, perhaps."

"With what conquests to her credit?"

"You would not expect me to know that? There were stories. As a young woman she was a kitchen-maid in one of the large houses on the outskirts of Cotter Bridge."

"Whose house?"

"I cannot remember the name."

And Kenworthy thought the lapse of memory was genuine.

"I cannot remember the name. The family has departed from the district years since. The man was a *parvenu*. He had made a fortune in the Potteries. He took this house, with a lavish retinue of servants, fought tooth and nail to get his family accepted into county society."

"Entertained lavishly?"

"With gross extravagance."

"So that Mrs. Booth had opportunity to observe ways of life that greatly attracted her?"

"There were, as I have said, stories. She clearly had her own methods of entering higher society."

"She must have been at least a little more attractive than she is now."

"That is as may be."

Horncastle was not prepared to enter into any spirit of semi-jocularity or cynicism. He answered as if he hated to sully his thoughts with the subject.

"You will understand, Superintendent, that I am recounting hearsay that is many decades old."

"What happened?" Kenworthy insisted.

Horncastle was almost short-tempered in his reply.

"I don't know what happened. There were stories. She had to leave."

"Pregnant?"

"I really could not say."

"Could that possibly be how Tommy was fathered?"

"That is out of the question. Tommy is thirty-nine. It was several years after she returned to Carrion Clough that his mother married. And Tommy was born in wedlock."

"What connection was there between Mrs. Booth and the Halliwells?" Kenworthy asked.

"I am not aware that there was any. It would greatly surprise me if there were."

"Mrs. Booth seems to bear malice towards the family."

"Superintendent, I think you would be wise to discount a great deal of what you hear in the village. Thomas John and his father were sadly misunderstood. It was assumed that throughout the negotiation with the Water Board they were prompted solely by motives of personal gain. But if those dispossessed cottagers and smallholders had had to deal directly with the Board, they would have fared a good deal worse than was in fact the case."

They came into the village of Anselm Norton: stone houses, a market square, a grocer's wholesaler's van, looking strangely improbable, with cardboard cartons of detergents stacked inside it.

Kenworthy changed the subject somewhat abruptly.

"How much land did the Drabbles own?"

Horncastle sighed impatiently.

"Superintendent, your passion for antiquity intrigues me.

It would be impertinent of me to suggest that mid-twentieth-century cupidity, passion, or envenomed relationships———"

"Nevertheless———," Kenworthy interrupted.

"Perhaps you could spare half an hour in Cotter Bridge, then, to come to my office."

And the sight of the small market-town, with its banks, its bus station and its old coaching hotel was another strange throw-back to civilization, to the long days of waiting before they had known anything of the case at all. Horncastle took them up noisy, lino-covered stairs to a cold office in which a coal fire had been laid but not lit, and went to the other side of a vast desk, stacked rather than littered with pink-taped bundles.

From within the knee-hole he brought a black, lacquered metal deed-box, which he unlocked with a key from his own ring. After some fumbling with papers, he produced a yellowed hand-drawn map, already splitting at the folds, and spread it out before them.

"Here you can see, gentlemen, the state of the valley before the construction of the dam."

He outlined red-bordered parcels of land with the tip of a silver propelling pencil.

"The Halliwells. The Drabbles. The Wardles. In a lesser way, the Haineses, the Penningtons."

"So the Penningtons owned land, too?"

"Miserable!" Horncastle said. "A couple of acres of poverty. Likewise the Orgills, the Farrows, the Hinchcliffes—names that you will no longer even find in the neighbourhood."

Kenworthy shifted the map on the desk so that he was looking at it squarely.

"So the Drabbles were the Halliwells' only serious competitors? The only ones with a significant stake to lose?

The only ones who, if they had had the capital, might have outbid Thomas John and his father."

Horncastle blew his nose noisily on an enormous white silk handkerchief.

"Superintendent, you did not know these days, and you did not know these people. What you are suggesting is unthinkable."

"Cagey old bar-steward!" Kenworthy said, as Judson was driving him back up the hill out of town. "Knows a bloody sight more about Mrs. Booth than he cares to let on. I wouldn't be surprised if he'd had her up against the wall of the butler's pantry himself, whilst the master was dropping aitches in the drawing-room."

Judson grunted.

"And look at the way he had all those documents about the take-over right at his finger-tips. Can't have had reasonable cause to look at those for donkeys' years. But my guess is he's had them out within the last week."

"Chief Constable wants a progress report first thing in the morning," Judson said.

"Yes. Well. We'll tell him about Ada Booth. And Caleb Wardle. And ask him what we can do about a man who won't let us bury him. I hope to heaven those two idle buggers have come up with something from Warburton Hall."

Wright and Russell were waiting in the parlour of the inn, sitting by an enormous blaze of fire, their faces red from the flames. From the way that Wright leapt to his feet when they entered, Kenworthy saw at once that something had gone badly.

"What's the matter? Made a pig's ear of it?" he asked brutally.

"We found the money, sir."

"Ah?"

"But I'm afraid . . ."

"Are you, indeed? All right, Sergeant, let's have it. Right from the start."

Wright began with the housekeeper at the Hall, and her denial that there had ever been a basket of washing. Kenworthy watched his discomfort without comment.

"So then we started looking for the car. If it hadn't been for Constable Russell, sir, we'd never have found it."

"Huh!"

"And it was a hell of a job digging it out."

"Huh!"

"When the burglar alarm went off, it was enough to make you do your nut."

"How much rhino was there?"

"We didn't count it, sir. We were bringing it down here."

"About how much?"

Wright looked helplessly at Russell.

"Difficult to tell, sir. Twelve hundred quid? No, that's just guessing. I don't know."

Kenworthy looked at him for some seconds in cold silence.

"We'll get it back, sir."

"You bloody well will," Kenworthy said.

Judson intervened, speaking directly to Russell.

"Just where did you spill it?"

"Over Henshaw Rocks, sir. You know the spot. It's a terrible drop."

Judson turned to Kenworthy.

"Not a hope, Superintendent, short of a mountain rescue team. Probably the stuff won't come to much harm while the frost's as severe as it is."

"And what's brother Calverley going to say when the mountain rescue team shows up here with his bloody basket? With no search warrant you break into his car. I've no doubt

you've dented his panels. You've interfered with the mecha-
nism. And you've thrown the family fortune over a bloody
cliff. All this to a bloke with a hot line to the Home
Secretary."

"I thought, sir, your instructions were——," Wright
began.

"My instructions are implicit. When you break the rules,
don't get found out."

"I wouldn't have thought, sir, there was much point in
finding the car unless we'd got into it."

"Well, what the hell do you think I sent you up there for?"

"Well, sir, I think you're being less than fair——"

"Fair, Sergeant Wright? Fair? Is this some bloody game
we're playing? With linesmen, and a referee? There's no
such thing as fair and unfair in police work, Sergeant.
There's success and failure. And you, my bonny bright lad,
have bloody well failed."

Wright did not meet his eyes.

"Haven't you?" Kenworthy hammered.

"Yes, sir."

"What have you?"

"Bloody well failed," Wright said shamefacedly.

"Still, I've no doubt they'll find some sort of employment
for you at the Yard. Indexing finger-prints, perhaps? Door-
man? Switch-board?"

"There is just one other thing, sir."

"Oh, God," Kenworthy said. "What now?"

"Well, sir, I think Constable Russell might prefer to tell
you himself."

Kenworthy looked from one to the other.

"Well, let's have it from one of you, anyway. Or are you
going to sing a bloody duet?"

"No, this is my pigeon, sir," Russell said. "That bit in the
newspaper . . ."

Russell stumbled through an attempt at self-justification, Judson's gaze drilling into his face. When he had finished, Kenworthy flopped histrionically into an armchair.

And he laughed. Uproariously and infectiously he guffawed, so that the other three looked at him first in consternation. And then a faint and uncertain smile appeared on Wright's face. Russell followed suit. Only Judson was unable to cope with the change of tension.

"Well, you bright couple of buggers! You pair of bright bloody stumers!"

He looked at his watch.

"Come next door. I'll buy you a pint apiece. God knows you must be ready for it."

◆ 17 ◆

Isaac Pennington was able to give them the latest news of Wilfred Wilson.

"They're going to keep him under observation for a few days. He isn't exactly on the danger list, as far as I could make out. You know how it is? They never tell you a bloody thing. But I reckon it'll be a month or so before they let him out, and I doubt if we'll see much of him up here after this."

Kenworthy patted Ben Drabble's elbow.

"Turn up for the book this is, then, Ben? The old so-and-so's got 'em beat."

Ben grinned sheepishly.

"Well, he always said he would."

Now it was all over, and he was back in the warm, with a well-charged pot in front of him, Ben seemed to have taken command of himself again. Or perhaps he had drunk fast and early. It was difficult to tell. At any rate he seemed more gay than he had been for days; and he was full of the cosmic significance of it all.

"Makes you bloody well think," he said.

Suddenly, Pennington called for silence, and turned up the

volume of the pre-war radio that stood on a shelf behind the bar.

The weather forecast: a rapid thaw was expected in all parts of the country within the next twenty-four hours.

"I thought it looked as if it was backing."

"A thaw can be a bigger bloody mess than a freeze-up."

"It doesn't want to move too bloody fast," Ben said. "There's a hell of a head of water in that top lodge."

Then unexpectedly the door opened, and Anthony Calverley came in, with a practised pleasant smile for them all and a request for a whisky that was heartfelt. He noticed their attention to the announcer's voice.

"What's this, then?"

"Thaw," someone said shortly.

"Thank God for that. Perhaps we shall have a thaw in more respects than one."

He looked at Kenworthy.

"Any progress, Superintendent? Or perhaps I shouldn't ask. What a hell of a day it's been. Any news of the schoolmaster?"

They told him. He seemed to be at pains to show his polite interest in their affairs. As a result of his conversation, they missed the first part of the news headlines. But suddenly he held up his hand for silence.

No; they had missed it. Something about government changes. A cabinet reshuffle. It did not matter much to Ben, Dick and Isaac. There was nothing, as there had been, once or twice of late, about Carrion Clough. But, the second time round, as the headlines were being expanded, Claverley rapped the counter smartly and commanded attention.

It was there: Mr. Anthony Calverley. At the mention of the name everybody listened. Half a sentence: a parenthetical clause. Calverley had been dropped from office. No explanation. Certainly no connection with the Clough. A few sentences about the new, up-and-coming figures. Routine changes. Then a gas-main that had burst in a Salford backstreet.

Calverley was dazed. Perhaps he had even been expecting promotion. Kenworthy watched him obliquely. The man was shattered. The great figure suddenly annulled, the future gone, the promise deflated. Calverley drained his glass and pushed it back for more.

So neither Kenworthy nor Judson saw the glance exchanged between Russell and Wright, the constable's beckoning inclination of the head that drew the sergeant away from the group.

It was minutes later that Kenworthy half turned.

"Come on, Shiner, it's time you bought . . ."

But Russell and Wright were no longer with them.

"Now what have those two young devils got into their heads?"

But Judson took their departure very seriously. He edged Kenworthy aside.

"I know what's got into Jim Russell's head. Bad lad makes good. We've got to stop them, Super."

"Those bloody rocks, you mean?"

"That money's all right while the frost holds. But if we get a mild wind from the west, the top snow will melt, even tonight. You can imagine what a bloody mess it will be, and what paper money will look like. I reckon they've gone to get it."

"Well, hell, let them. I know I was a bit rough with Shiner. But when all's said and done, they did make a dog's dinner of it."

"Superintendent, you don't know what conditions are like. And at night, too."

"There's a moon," Kenworthy said.

"Has Wright any experience of climbing?"

"Not to my knowledge."

"I'm pretty sure Russell hasn't."

"They can look after themselves," Kenworthy said. "And if they pull it off, we're out of the pooh."

Judson passed his hand over his forehead.

"Superintendent, I can't make you out. One minute you're all sympathy, the next you're as hard as nails. Come the dawn, we shall have a couple of dead coppers to account for."

Kenworthy hesitated.

"What do you suggest we do, then? Go after them? They're younger men than we are, Judson. They've got a start on us."

"I'll alert mountain rescue," Judson said. "But I wouldn't care for one of them to fracture a pelvis."

"Leave it!" Kenworthy said. "We're only surmising. We don't know for certain that they've gone. And if we call out mountain rescue and somebody gets hurt—for nothing . . ."

"I've got a responsibility for a member of my own force."

"I said leave it!" Kenworthy said. "Let me buy you another drink."

But neither man was interested in drinking. They sat for a while neither talking nor touching their glasses, lost in two separate and very different reveries.

Kenworthy was the first to speak.

"You know, Judson, there's a picture that I can't get out of my mind: Tommy Booth after he'd been sacked from the farm, coming down the hill in the late afternoon, and meeting this unknown character coming up. And Tommy would have spoken to him, wouldn't he?

"'Good afternoon, Mr. Shelmerdine,' he'd say, wouldn't he? I can't help feeling, you know, that those are the words that would loosen the whole dam. 'Good afternoon, Mr. Shelmerdine,' we say to some bright character. His eyes flicker, and we've got him."

But Judson was not impressed. There was no longer any enchantment in working with the man from London. Judson had his own problems, his own professional morality.

"Do you encourage your sergeants," he asked, "to go swanning off in the middle of a case, without a by-your-leave, without even saying where they're going?"

"If they bring the bacon home," Kenworthy said. "If they make a mess of it, I chuck the book at them."

"Do you understand, Superintendent, just what they're up against out there tonight?"

"I'm trying hard not to think about it," Kenworthy said. "I'm not quite such a heartless bugger as you think. We couldn't have *ordered* them up the hill, could we?"

"And wouldn't."

"But if they pull it off, Judson . . ."

"Cat in hell's chance."

"It isn't just the money, Judson."

"I'm not worried about the money."

"Somebody had better be. But there's more to it than that. Margaret Halliwell wouldn't have taken the family treasury up the hill without a word of explanation, would she? In that basket, Judson, there'd be a covering letter, something that'll tell us a good deal more than she ever intended to!"

"You're forgetting that she originally intended to deliver the goods in person."

Calverley left the bar and walked past them towards the door.

"Good night, Mr. Shelmerdine," Kenworthy said. Calverley looked at him as if he were mad.

"No, Judson. There'll be a letter."

Judson pushed away a pint from which he had taken no more than the foam.

"There are two or three jobs I ought to be doing in Cotter Bridge. Unless you really need me here."'

Kenworthy nodded vaguely, dismissing him. Then he finished his own drink, slowly and with no relish, fetched his hat, scarf and gloves, and went out into the night.

He paused at the bottom of the lane that led to the farm, looking about him, appearing to measure distances in the snow, allowing his eyes to accustom themselves to the shadows. Presently he walked resolutely into the hamlet and knocked on the door of the Booths' cottage.

Mrs. Booth let him in without much delay, apparently not at all surprised to see him.

The living-room was lit only by an oil lamp, which smelled rancid and overpowering, and Tommy was sitting in a corner, poring over a nineteenth-century book of Grand Tour pictures.

"I've come for another look at your scrapbook," Kenworthy said, eliminating small talk, and at once the woman went to the cupboard and handed him the bulky volume. He turned back in time to the opening of the dam. The factual account of the laying of the foundation stone was there. But where the photograph of the platform party had been, there was a blank half-page. The newsprint had been roughly scraped out, and in one place a hole had been scored in the paper of the album.

He looked at her intently, and she returned his gaze with silent satisfaction.

What sort of a beauty could she possibly have been in her late teens? A mere slip of a girl in her kitchen-maid days, no doubt. Firmer lines, certainly; clothes that fitted trimly; eyes now almost stagnant, that might have been langorous as bait.

"Very silly of you," he said.

Genuine amusement flitted across her features.

"Just making a nuisance of yourself, or trying to protect someone?" he asked. "You're wasting your time, you know.

Your friend Shelmerdine's face is pretty well etched on my memory."

She smiled esoterically.

Your friend Shelmerdine . . .

Could it have been Sherlmerdine who had thought he was seducing her at one of the house-parties? And if so, how the hell could it help? It wasn't Shelmerdine himself who had gone up to the farm. Shelmerdine was long dead.

So?

Kenworthy idly turned back the pages of the album. There was an account of a grouse-shoot on the moors: a brace of baronets, the characteristic round of lavish entertainment. Ada Booth, or whatever her name used to be, would have packed their sandwiches, plucked the birds for the table, made eyes covertly at some over-sexed young house-guest, whiling away his boredom in a mausoleum of a villa in the last outpost of the Pennines.

"Did you ever work at Warburton Hall?" Kenworthy asked.

She shook her head.

"Didn't you ever want to?"

"Why should I?"

"I thought that sort of life appealed to you."

There was a page of photographs of ballroom groups: bustles. Probably the crinoline had died late in Cotter Bridge.

"Did you ever try any of those dresses on?"

She came closer, to see what he was looking at.

"Why should I want to try *them* on? I'd dresses of my own."

"Who are these people, anyway?"

She beckoned to Tommy.

"Come over here and tell him."

And Tommy's black finger-nail went from face to face on the page, his eyes glistening with pride as he picked out one after the other.

"Sir William Anstruther, Mr. Michael Woolf, Lady Anstruther, The Right Honourable J. Arthur Beasley, Mrs. Amelia Woolf . . ."

Mrs. Booth preened herself, like a teacher presenting the stilted antics of a well-drilled child. Tommy was thirty-nine.

"I'm going to ask you if I may borrow this."

She picked up the book and held it flat against her bosom.

"You're not having it."

"I'm not impounding it, Mrs. Booth. You'll get it back. I'll give you a receipt for it."

"No!"

Her obstinacy brought out something elemental in her. There was a glint of the wild cat in her eyes.

"If I have to come back with a warrant for it, we might have to keep it a long time. I only want it for a few hours."

"No!"

"In that case I'm going to have to ask Tommy to come with me."

"What for? Where to?"

"Only down to Cotter Bridge. For further questioning."

He knew he had beaten her.

"You've no right," she said.

"On the contrary."

"There's nothing in there that will help you."

"I'll bring it back first thing in the morning, I promise you."

"No!"

"Get your cap, Tommy. And you'll need your razor, your shaving-brush——"

She spat a mouthful of obscenities, then thrust the book into his hands.

He lost no time in letting himself out of the cottage. She made no move to open the door for him. And a trickle of saliva was running from a corner of Tommy's mouth as he looked across the room with shared hatred.

Kenworthy paused for a moment to take in the night again: a dazzling whiteness of the moon against the snow, the familiar crackle underfoot. It was only a few tens of yards to the bank of the reservoir. He went and stood and looked out across the ice, out where Wright and Russell were risking life and limb. It reminded him of Holland during the war, when they were bogged down in the mists of the Maas, and a line of dim trees in the middle distance represented the end of the known world. Then he heard a crunch of boots in the snow. Someone was coming down the lane, walking in the direction where no more houses lay, a dark, featureless silhouette, striding purposefully.

Kenworthy waited motionless until the figure had drawn almost abreast of him. Then he stepped suddenly from the shadow of the wall.

"Goodnight, Mr. Shelmerdine!"

With long, stumbling steps the figure began to run, then fell headlong in the snow.

·18·

Wright and Russell skirted the edge of the reservoir.

"Let's hope the ice holds," Wright said.

"Holds? Man, it's five feet thick!"

"I wish we had some gear. Ropes and what-not."

"You ever done any climbing? You know how to use a rope?"

"No. Do you?"

"No."

"We're bloody mad," Wright said.

"We'll be bloody mad if Calverley holds us to account for twelve hundred quid, or whatever it was. Feel that wind? It's changed. That money will be pulp by morning."

Russell swung his entrenching tool.

"I reckon I can cut steps in the ice with this."

"I ought to say no to the whole idea, Jim. But we're in it up to the eye-balls. We can but try. If we've lost that basket, we're for the high jump."

"Let's get cracking, then. When we get there, we'll play it as it comes."

They plunged across the snow-covered ice, wearing their

snow-shoes again, following a long straight line across the waist of the reservoir. At least, they hoped they were following a straight line, but every now and then, when they stopped to examine their wake, they found they were veering to their left.

"It doesn't matter much where we hit the other bank. Just a bit further to walk when we get to the other side, that's all."

There was enough moon for them to see where they were going, and the hulk of the distant hill loomed up where the bowl of stars ended. The sky was black, and the great bear was standing on his tail.

"Does Kenworthy think he's going to get to the bottom of this one?"

"He will," Wright said.

"I'm damned if I can understand his line of thought. It strikes me he's paying more attention to museum-pieces than he is to evidence."

"It's all evidence to Kenworthy."

"I don't go for all this roots-in-the-Crimea stuff, myself."

"Kenworthy's looking for motive," Wright said. "He thinks the motive's buried right under where we're walking now."

"If you ask me, the motive's what we tipped out of that bloody basket."

"All the more reason for getting it back."

They pressed forward. But it was a long walk, and every step cost an effort in itself. It was well over a quarter of a mile of straight line. The distance before them seemed to grow no less and the stretch behind them no more.

At length, however, they reached the scattered boulders of the further shore. They clambered over them and found it difficult in places to differentiate between solid rock and heaped snow.

Russell stopped to take his bearings.

"First bit's going to be a rough old scramble. Hard going, but not really dangerous till we strike the bare rock higher up. And we ought to start keeping our eyes peeled. Some of it could have tumbled down as far as this."

Wright switched on his torch, which he was trying to conserve as much as he could. But there was no sign of anything in the snow except the footprints of a few unidentified birds.

"The stuff might have scattered over a hell of an area. There might be bundles of notes half a mile apart."

"There might, but I don't think there will. Most of it would lodge pretty close to where it landed. Anyway, I'm not to ten quid either way, are you?"

"I'll settle for eleven hundred and ninety."

"Up there, then!"

It was hands and knees up a slope of seventy degrees, cold wet snow thrust up their sleeves. Once or twice Wright slipped back a yard or two, but Russell was surer-footed and was waiting at the first resting-place to give the sergeant a hand.

It was a narrow ledge, fronting to a concave rock shelter, so situated that there were a few square yards completely free from snow. Wright swung the disc of his torch and saw loose stones, a bleached broken twig, the roots of a hawthorn drawing sustenance from an impossibly impoverished cranny in the rocks. And ice bulged over the rock in shining globules.

Wright looked down the slope they had climbed and scanned it casually with his torch.

"Jim! Down there!"

There was a wad of pound notes, almost end on in the snow, ten yards below them, and to the right of the route they had taken. Both men scrambled, slipping, falling, rolling. And when they reached the spot, the notes were frozen into the snow, so solid that they crackled like tinder.

Russell hacked about them with his entrenching tool. Wright picked up the bundle and thrust it into his pocket. A few feet away they found a bag of sovereigns. And that was all.

"The rest's higher up," Russell said. "I thought as much. It's lying not so far from where we set eyes on it."

He clambered back to the ledge, stood back and examined the rock face above him.

"So near and yet so far. The whole lot's less than the length of a cricket-pitch away from us."

He chose a spot at chest level and began to hack at the ice.

"You're not going to try to get up there?"

"That's what we've come for, isn't it?"

"You'll break your neck."

"I've been up here often enough when I was a lad."

"You're not a lad now. And you've not been up here at night, on the bloody ice."

Russell tested with the tip of his toes the narrow step he had cut.

"Here! Get hold of my other foot. Hold me while I cut a hand-hold."

The edge of his boot was cruelly sharp against Wright's hand. For what seemed an unconscionable time, Wright took his weight, then Russell swung himself against the rock face and supported himself.

"All right, Shiner?"

"I'm all right. I should worry."

"If I can do one bit, I can do another."

Russell flailed at the ice, eventually pulled himself another five feet higher. Wright tried to follow him, found that he could get no sort of grip in Russell's steps.

"Better not try it," Russell said. "It's years since I was up here, but it's all coming back to me."

Wright turned his back to the rock, pulled off his gloves and blew into his hands. He felt useless now, and every minute's delay convinced him that Russell was dicing with death. Suddenly there was a scrabbling and Russell cursed without inhibition. His foot had slipped, but he appeared to have hung on with his arms.

"Give it up, Jim!"

Russell replied in terms of Anglo-Saxon anatomy.

"You've only got Kenworthy to reckon with. I'm up against Judson, too."

Wright heard the drag of his clothing against the rock face. Then Russell looked down and spoke with panting excitement.

"I can see it, Shiner! Perched right on the edge. And I reckon most of the stuff's still in it."

More scraping of boot-irons against the stone. And then:

"I can just reach it. But I don't know how I'm going to get it down. Damn it, I need another pair of arms."

Wright made another attempt to climb up the first stage, and this time managed to raise himself precariously his own height above the ledge. He badly needed his torch, but both arms were immobilized, holding himself in position.

Snow suddenly avalanched past him, covering his shoulders with surprising weight.

"What the hell?" he shouted.

"Not to worry," came from above. "I can't reach the basket, but I'm going to undermine it, dig a chute for it. I'll let it slide right down. You'd better get back where you came from. And stick well into the shelter."

Wright jumped and slithered back on to the ledge. The avalanche continued. And then the basket came over the edge, catching him on the face and shoulder and ricocheting down into the bank of snow below him. And at the same moment Russell lost his grip, swore primitively and fell heavily on to the ledge, landing on an edge of rock with a thump that knocked the breath out of his chest.

"You O.K., Jim?"

"Yes. I'll be up in a minute."

But he was not. He tried to push himself up on his elbows, but sank back with a groan.

"God, Jim! I hope you haven't broken anything."

"I reckon I've broken everything, mate."

• 19 •

KENWORTHY HAD BEEN on the point of hurling himself in a rugger tackle on the man who reacted to the name of Shelmerdine, but the figure lay full length in the snow and showed no signs of aggression when the superintendent came up to him. Only fear, cowering on the ground, blubbering incoherently and trying half to roll, half to crawl away.

Kenworthy gripped him firmly by the shoulders.

"God's sake get a grip of yourself, man."

It was Ben Drabble. The waterman was writhing as if he really thought he was being assailed by a ghost from the past.

"It's me, Kenworthy. Be your age, man. You'll come to no harm."

Or would he? Was it fear of ghosts, or of a devastating witness?

"Kenworthy?"

"Yes. Let me help you up."

Drabble struggled to his feet.

"God, you gave me a scare. I thought you were—"

"Yes?"

"I didn't know who the hell you were. That name, Shelmerdine, I haven't heard it mentioned for years and years."

Drabble dusted snow from his clothes and rubbed his right hip, on which he had landed heavily.

"What right have you to be hanging about in the dark putting the fear of God into law-abiding citizens?"

"Where are *you* off to, anyway, in this direction, and at this time of night?" Kenworthy asked.

"To the dam, of course. What the hell?"

"You've got business at the dam, in the dark? Something that won't wait till tomorrow?"

"You bloody town people," Drabble said. "You don't know what it's all about, do you? Didn't you hear on the radio, there's going to be a thaw tomorrow?"

"Yes. I suppose that'll give you work to do."

"Work to do? Work to do?"

Ben Drabble was not accustomed to civilized tempering of his wrath.

"Listen! Perhaps you can talk some sense into them for me. Eight bloody times I've rung up Head Office, and told them the state the masonry is in. Has any bugger been out to see it? Do they take any bloody notice of me? Do you know what's going to happen when the ice melts in those cracks? Do you know the whole bloody dam's going to crack? And with the head of water there is, it'll flood the valley up to twenty feet. But of course, I'm only the maintenance man. They take not a blind bit of notice of me. And as to coming out to see for themselves—bit too flaming cold for them, I reckon."

It occurred to Kenworthy that perhaps Ben had cried wolf once too often.

"So you're going to the dam?"

"It's my job to be there, isn't it?"

"Is there anything useful you can do there?"

"What do you think? This needs a building team. Concrete mixers, steel reinforcement. I don't know how they're going to hold it."

"I'll come with you," Kenworthy said.

And they walked together along the frozen lane, climbed a low wall beside a padlocked gate which Drabble did not bother to open, and went into the little hut that he used as his HQ. It was sparsely furnished with a wooden table and an armchair with a scraggy, filthy cushion. The office equipment was of the most rudimentary: a calendar, a time-sheet and a correspondence tray cut out of an old Home Guard petrol tin. Against one wall were leaning the equally primitive tools of Drabble's trade: crowbars, drain-rods and a spade.

Drabble picked up his telephone, a chipped, dirty instrument on one corner of the table, and carried on a long, loud and bitter conversation with someone who Kenworthy gathered was a night-duty engineer.

Kenworthy turned over the pages of Mrs. Booth's album: a meeting of the hunt outside a pub in Anselm Norton; the planting of memorial saplings for the coronation of George V; a long list of casualties from Hazebrouck and Ypres. In the later years, after the end of the twenties, little had been pasted in—only an occasional obituary, and the visit of very minor royalty to Cotter Bridge.

"Listen, I've got a police superintendent here. I'll put *him* on to you."

And Ben thrust the receiver into Kenworthy's hand.

"Tell him! *You* tell him!"

Kenworthy sought for words.

"Our friend here seems distinctly worried."

"Yes, well tell him we'll be along first thing in the

morning. There's nothing we could do tonight, even if things are as bad as he seems to think."

"Well, I don't know anything about it, of course, but—"

"We've had all this before, Superintendent. A few bricks come away in the culvert. Bound to happen with the sort of frost we've been having. Happens every year. No harm in it."

Ben was making urgent gestures.

"Mr. Drabble seems to think—"

"I've already given the foreman-ganger his instructions. They'll be on the spot at first light in the morning. And nothing could happen before then. Believe me, Superintendent, nothing short of a block buster could crack that concrete."

Kenworthy hung up. Ben put a match to an ancient paraffin heater.

"No go?"

"He seems to think you're being over-anxious, Ben."

"He just doesn't bloody well want to know."

Ben came up to the corner of the table and glanced casually at the album.

"If I were a superstitious man," he said, and Kenworthy forbore to smile, "I'd say the old man had got into the dam itself. That was a right bloody turn-up at the cemetery, wasn't it?"

"That's how legends are born, Ben."

"What's all this about Shelmerdine, anyway? You nearly scared me out of my wits."

"You knew Shelmerdine, did you?"

"Hell, no. He was before my time. I've seen a picture of him in the Board's Office."

"So you'd recognize him again if you saw him?"

Ben looked at him with a fresh trace of fear.

"That's not bloody likely, is it? He died—"

"I mean somebody like him, somebody who might be mistaken for him."

"Search me!" Ben said. "I don't know anyone who looks like Shelmerdine. What *is* this all about?"

Ben was being utterly natural. Kenworthy wrote him off. If he had been the man whom Tommy Booth had seen, his answers now would have been vastly different. Kenworthy nodded towards the album.

"A lot in there that would interest you."

Ben turned a page or two.

"Yes, by heaven, this takes you back. Where did you get this?"

"Ada Booth."

"Aye," Ben said. "Sets a lot of store by the old days, does Ada."

"Got good reason to, perhaps?"

"She used to have a lot of jumped-up bloody ideas. Till she found she couldn't do it on thirty bob a week."

"Know much about her?"

"Not a woman I have anything to do with, or would want to. Supposed to have got herself in the family way in Cotter Bridge and had to come back here. And there's some say that Tommy was a love-child, and that's why her husband left her."

"So she went wrong twice, then?"

"Was she ever anything but wrong?"

"I mean, could it have been the same man in both cases?"

"Damned if I know. I never dipped my candle in that grease."

"It seems to have been an uncommonly well-kept secret," Kenworthy persisted. "There must have been plenty of theories in Carrion Clough."

"Aye, but Carrion Clough isn't Cotter Bridge. Different

set of folk altogether. Big stuff in Cotter Bridge, you know, Superintendent."

Kenworthy thought of the seedy hotel, the diminutive bus-station, the microcosm of a Woolworth's. And yet Cotter Bridge had always seemed like the big city to the Clough-dwellers.

"These folk, for instance . . ."

Ben had reached the photograph of the ball-room group whose names Tommy Booth had recited with juvenile pride.

"Amelia Woolf, here, I only knew her when she was an old woman."

"Which is Amelia Woolf?"

"This one. They had a big house halfway to Cotter Green. Came from the Potteries."

Ben was pointing to the woman in the middle of the group.

"That's not Amelia Woolf!"

"It bloody is!"

Ben looked at him with incipient truculence. But Kenworthy was remembering, face by face, the names as Tommy Booth had pronounced them from left to right: Sir William Anstruther, Mr. Michael Woolf, Lady Anstruther, the Right Honourable J. Arthur Beasley, Mrs. Amelia Woolf . . .

"Who's this, then?"

Kenworthy's finger rested on the woman at the end of the line.

"Don't know."

"How many of these people do you know?"

"Only Mrs. Woolf. And Mr. Beasley—he used to be our M.P."

"Which is Mr. Beasley?"

Ben indicated the man whom Tommy had called Anstruther.

Kenworthy thumped the table.

"By heaven, Ben, we're there!"

He could see what had happened. He knew now why Mrs. Booth had torn out the photograph of the group at the dam. Tommy's memory was quite phenomenal, but his brain was clogged and unreliable. He remembered things all right, but he had the wrong associations. He thought Mrs. Woolf was Lady Anstruther. And the man he thought was Mr. Shelmerdine was someone else: someone who was neither six foot three nor sad and distinguished looking.

He reached for Ben's telephone.

"Hullo? Give me Cotter Bridge police station, please."

It happened sometimes with children. They got hold of wrong ideas, and persisted sometimes in them for years. *Lead me not into Thames Station.*

"Could I speak to Inspector Judson, please? And if he isn't in the station, would you put me through to his home, please?"

Someone whom Ada Booth, who was quick-witted enough to see that Kenworthy must not be allowed to see that photograph again, was leaning over backwards to protect.

Judson was still in his office.

"Evening, Inspector. No, no, they haven't come back yet.—No, I've still no idea.—Oh, don't worry about them, Inspector, they'll be all right.—Listen, Inspector, before you come up here in the morning, I want you to call in the *Advertiser* offices. And borrow their back-number file for . . ." he flicked over the pages of the album, ". . . Yes, that's right—for 1901. Goodnight, Inspector."

He replaced the receiver and went over to warm his hands in front of the mica window of Ben's oil-heater. He found Judson's mixture of consternation, disbelief and exasperation extremely amusing.

✦ 20 ✦

KENWORTHY RETURNED TO the Legless Volunteer in time to see the last customer leaving the front door. He told the Penningtons he expected to be up late, and Isaac put more coal on the fire of the room that they had been using as a sitting-room. Kenworthy sat by it and smoked.

He was certain now who had done it. But he was not sure why, though he thought he could guess, and there was a multitude of details about the comings and goings of it that he simply did not know. And it all had to be known, for without it there could be no proof. And without an assurance of proof, a premature confrontation could sabotage the whole issue. A false move now, and the murderer could cover up his tracks and live out his natural life in freedom with impunity.

It was a stage of case-work that Kenworthy loathed. Gazing into the fire, watching a yellow jet of flame lapping the black edges of a coal, he remembered other instances: bringing a suspect down on an all-night train from Newcastle, probing questions in a locked first-class compartment, and the dawning realization from station after station—

Retford, Grantham, Peterborough, Hatfield—that before they reached King's Cross he was going to have to change his mind. And another train, skirting a filthy little north country canal, bursting with simulated self-confidence, wondering whether the killer of a local bigwig was going to keep a confidence-trick appointment at the next stop.

It was all a matter of stage-management. How to stage-manage this one?

The Penningtons were in the room, without asking whether he minded their incursion on his privacy. Damn it, it was their room, wasn't it? Cold beef and pickled onions for their very late supper. And of course, an invitation to join them, which they did not press when he politely declined.

The yellow jet spluttered out, high pressure smoke fizzing out from the same spot. What was he doing it for? A bitter hatred of vice and crime for their own sake? A poetical desire to avenge this rather lovely woman who had paid vicariously for the sins of her ancestors? Or just the love of personal triumph, arriving back at the Yard, Kenworthy's done it again?

Kenworthy suddenly felt sick. He always did on the last lap, when the stark possibility of ignominious failure was lurking for him round the last corner.

Pennington spoke with his mouth full of wholemeal bread and pickles.

"The other two are out late."

Kenworthy grunted, rudely in spite of himself.

"Be a bit better in a couple of days," Pennington said. "Be able to come and go as we please again."

A couple of days: Carrion Clough would be in proper contact with the world again. Calverley would be back in London, sparkling with political epigrams, scrabbling again at the bottom of the ladder. His mother would be safely returned to the fringes of his existence, sipping raw-nosed at

the communion cup on cold, foggy mornings. Wilfred
Wilson would be on the road to convalescence, itching to
get back to his daily round, and the process of killing
himself at the bar of the Volunteer. The day after tomorrow
the gathering grounds would have given up their own.
Tomorrow was the last day. Tomorrow he had to seal
everything off.

"Where have those two gone at this time of night, then?"
Pennington asked bluntly.

Damn it, did they think he was made of stone? Weren't
Wright and Russell grown men, capable of making their
own decisions and taking their own calculated risks? Hadn't
he taken chances of his own in his early days? And where
the hell were Wright and Russell, anyway? They'd been
gone four hours.

"Out on inquiries," Kenworthy answered gruffly.

"You policemen," Martha Pennington said diplomati-
cally. "The hours you have to work."

Then there was a thunderous banging on the outside door.
Kenworthy started in his chair. Pennington caught his fork
against the side of his plate and shuffled across the room in
his carpet-slippers. He returned almost at once, accompanied by three big men, in gaily coloured woollen caps with
furry bobs on top, and with hose-tops turned over the edges
of their boots. One of them had an alpine rope coiled about
his shoulder and waist.

"Mountain rescue," he said. "Inspector Judson asked me
to tell you that this is absolutely unofficial."

"Glad to see you," Kenworthy said.

"Henshaw Rocks, isn't it?" the leader asked.

"That's what they called it."

And Pennington caught his breath shamelessly.

"They've not gone climbing Henshaw Rocks tonight?"
Kenworthy ignored him.

"You'll have no difficulty in following their footsteps, I'm sure."

But before there could be any more talk, there was imperative knocking on the door again. Pennington let Wright in, and the sergeant sized up the newcomers immediately and with unconcealed relief.

"Thank God you lot are here."

"Accident?" Kenworthy asked.

Wright nodded.

"How bad?"

"It's Russell."

"Of course, I know it's Russell. Who the hell else? Father Christmas?"

"I think he's broken his back, sir. Can't move from the waist down."

"I hope you left him warm enough."

Wright flapped his jacket open.

"There's my coat on him, as well as his own."

Already the rescue team were out of the door, clambering into a battered old van. Wright made to join them.

"No need for you to go, Shiner. Come here and put me in the picture."

Wright was blue with cold. Kenworthy sent Pennington for rum for him. The sergeant gave a staccato statement of events.

"So you got the basket?"

"Sir."

"And it's still up there?"

"Yes, sir. I thought of bringing it, but it would have slowed me up terribly."

"Don't keep excusing yourself, Sergeant. I know bloody well why you didn't bring it. I'm just checking on the facts. Nip after them and make sure they bring it down, will you? They can only take the van as far as the dam."

Wright hurried to the door.

"And Shiner . . ."

"Sir?"

"Don't make it sound too bloody callous."

Kenworthy telephoned for an ambulance to be waiting at the inn. And when Wright returned, he sat him by the fire and quizzed him with conscious patience about the details of the expedition.

"But it's a bloody pity about Russell, sir. A damned good copper."

"Let's just wait and see how bad it is, Shiner."

And then, after a lapse of silence.

"At least, it gives us a good excuse to overlook two bits of forgetfulness in his recent career."

Pennington came and joined them by the hearth.

"Missus is getting some hot soup on."

He said no more about Henshaw Rocks, and was studiously careful not to ask any questions. An hour later the ambulance arrived, its attendants asking things they could not answer about the probable nature of the injuries.

It was four a.m. before they heard the van pull up outside, and then there was the movement of a collapsible stretcher from one vehicle to the other.

"How serious?" Kenworthy asked.

"Hard to tell. No obvious fracture. But he's taken a hell of a thump."

"Shock?"

"As you might expect. But he's got guts, that lad."

Only then was the basket brought in. And as the rescuers were bowed over bowls of Martha's bodisome stew, Wright began counting out bundles of notes and stacks of golden sovereigns on the corner of the table.

Kenworthy watched him keenly, but without interfering.

The rescuers were clearly curious, but their leader bustled them out.

"Some of us have got a day's work to do tomorrow."

"How much?"

"£1,350, give or take fifty or so. There's another wad in the pocket of my coat, on Russell. And I'm pretty sure we didn't pick it all up."

"No note of any kind?"

The bottom of the basket was bare.

"No, sir."

"I'm pretty sure there is a covering letter."

Wright repeated the argument Judson had used.

"She had originally intended to hand it over directly to the housekeeper. There wouldn't be any need."

"I *know* there's a letter, Shiner. There bloody well *has* to be."

Wright did not comment. It was unlike Kenworthy to indulge in wishful thinking.

"I mean, she'd just have a word or two with the housekeeper about it, wouldn't she? But she'd have to put something on paper, for the sake of the Commander and his wife when they returned. Only common courtesy, isn't it?"

And what if there were a letter, Wright thought. *Please look after this little lot, till the shower have gone back home.* How was that likely to help?

"Over what sort of an area was the spondulicks scattered?" Kenworthy wanted to know.

"Difficult to tell, sir, in the dark. Nothing more than about thirty yards from where I left Russell, I should think."

"And it all came down the cliff. There wouldn't be any left on top, would there?"

"That's as near enough a dead cert, sir. Russell started a hell of an avalanche."

"And any letter there was would be on top of the basket,

wouldn't it? Do you remember seeing one, when you first found it?"

"I can't say I do, sir. But I only gave it the most cursory glance."

"What I'm getting at, Shiner, is that she wouldn't leave a letter where all the rhino had to be unloaded before it was found, would she? She'd want the letter to come out first, wouldn't she? Tucked in at the side, perhaps, but with at least a corner of the envelope visible at first sight?"

"Could well be, sir."

Wright did not believe it. But the old man had got this letter thoroughly up his nose. It wouldn't pay to dash his hopes too wildly to the ground.

"So it would be one of the first things to fall out, wouldn't it, Shiner?"

"In theory, sir."

"This isn't theory, Shiner. It's elementary physics. Somewhere up on that slope there's an envelope. And in that envelope there's a message; Margaret Halliwell telling us—though not in so many words, mark you—who was going to kill her."

"You know something, don't you, sir?"

"I know damn all, Shiner. I only know it was a damned clever move on Margaret Halliwell's part to get that cash up to the Hall. The sort of move old Thomas John might have thought up himself. And if she was clever enough for that, she'd have been clever enough to blaze us a bit of a trail. Just in case."

"Could be, sir."

"And by halfway through tomorrow morning, that letter's going to be soggy and illegible."

He looked at his watch, and then at Pennington.

"Feel like a walk up Henshaw Rocks, Isaac?"

It was his first attempt at heavy jocularity for several

hours, and Pennington could only take it in heavy earnest. His eyes were afraid, and he could not think at once of a way out.

Kenworthy laughed. He was on the brink of action again, had something positive to do.

"Skip it, Isaac. We can cope. But the least you can do is lend Shiner your overcoat. He'll catch his death, else."

·21·

WHEN WRIGHT AWOKE it was to the sound of water, steadily dripping somewhere outside. And when he went to the window, and wiped it clear of condensation, he saw that the snow had softened on the eaves, and a slow but constant trickle was falling from the gutter of a corrugated iron lean-to.

Not for the first time in his work with Kenworthy, the superintendent had sent him to bed nearer seven than six in the morning, with the injunction that an hour's sleep was infinitely preferable to none at all: and that there was the very hell of a day ahead of them.

Wright did not wait for hot water. He shaved in cold, tearing at the bristles on his chin with a blade that seemed to have the edge of a saw.

They had traipsed through the snow, crossing the by now well-trodden track across the reservoir at a speed set by Kenworthy himself. Although no longer a young man, the superintendent seemed to be driven by some internal engine that worked with whip-cord and steel wheels. Even Wright and Russell had halted once or twice on their way across, but not Kenworthy. Kenworthy leaned forward, into the wind, and pushed himself on like the stroke of an eight impelling a tired crew.

When they reached the foot of the bank down which the basket had rolled, they searched at first for a quarter of an hour in vain. Then Wright was the first to strike ore, literally so, for he picked up a half-sovereign, which he announced without triumph. Kenworthy, ranging widely on the perimeter of the area, was the first to find bank-notes, and he shouted the news across seventy yards of cold, white waste. Then he disappeared over the rim of the bank, plunging his legs into snow with utter abandon. Wright was left to deal with a relatively barren area. Near where he had found the first coin he eventually picked up three more, and then the full bag from which they spilled.

And then Kenworthy shouted jubilantly across the empty night, his voice echoing against the walls of snow rather as Calverley's klaxon had done.

"This is it, Shiner."

Wright threw himself stumbling across the drifts, and came upon Kenworthy reading a sheaf of papers by the light of his torch.

"Good girl!" he was saying. "Good girl! You knew, didn't you? You knew! She knew, Shiner. She *knew*."

Kenworthy was back to mischievous mystification. Or perhaps it was not even mischievous. Perhaps he was still not wholly sure of himself and did not want to give this away in conversation. At any rate, he showed no inclination to talk or think aloud. He simply stuffed Margaret's papers into his pocket, made a ludicrously unsuccessful attempt at a glissade down the bank towards their homeward track, and strode out along it even faster than they had come. Kenworthy was in ebullient mood. Only once did he speak, and that was when, in spite of his partly stimulated vigour, he had to stop to rest.

"Know any French, Shiner?"

"Never my strongest subject, sir."

"Know what *mise en scène* means?"

"It must be your pronunciation, sir."

"That's what's been worrying me, Shiner—the *mise en scène*. How the blazes to stage the last act. And damn me if she hasn't set it up for us."

"Glad to hear it, sir."

But Kenworthy told him no more, did not even, as he had half expected, try to teach him object lessons by interrogating him about whatever theories he might hold himself.

When they got back to the Legless Volunteer, where Pennington had been sleeping fully dressed in the living-room, ready to let them in, Kenworthy ordered Wright to bed. And when Wright came down to breakfast, late and hurried, it was evident from the superintendent's stubble beard and puffy eyes that Kenworthy had not been to bed at all.

"Ah! Shiner! There you are! Rested?"

Wright saw at once that there was a good deal of activity in and about the inn. Doors kept opening and closing. Men—all of them strangers—were coming and going. Kenworthy seemed to be playing no part in it.

"This is the beginning of the last act, sir?"

"This? Hell, no. Newspaper reporters, engineers. The bloody dam's bust, Shiner."

But he said it casually, as if he had been announcing that it looked like rain.

"Bust?"

"Ben Drabble thinks the old man's got into the stone-work. Several hundred million gallons of Corporation water about to irrigate the valley."

"Good God, sir. Then we shall have to——"

"We shall have to do bugger all about it, Shiner, except steer well clear of the whole issue. Never mind what anybody says. We've got our own work to do."

"There are people living in that valley, sir."

"I know. And Master Anthony's down there on a borrowed motor-bike, doing all the necessary heroics. Stopping to pose for a photograph now and then, no doubt, with his feet in a puddle. Oddly enough, it's the same reporter who produced the milk-maid yarn, who's now going to plaster the banner headlines about the gallant swashbuckler. TV and what-not will be here before the morning's out. Do Calverley a hell of a lot of good."

"Good for him!"

"Good for nothing! It's only a trickle as yet. With any luck they'll plug the breach in time. It'll only get really nasty when the thaw bites deep. Up to now it's not much worse than a bloody mess. All Calverley's doing is going round warning them at the farms, and if I know anything about these people, they've been expecting this for days. Still, it's young hopeful's best chance of a public comeback. I'll not begrudge it him. And we shall have the national boys here in time for our final curtain."

"All laid on, is it, sir—the *mise en scène*?"

"Judson's doing a lot of spade-work. God bless him. I don't think he really liked being rung in his bed at half past six, but if I'm up, I don't see why any county inspector should sleep. And I've plenty for you to do, too. I want a gathering of the clans at Moss Hill Farm. At two o'clock prompt. You're responsible for getting them there. All of them. Ben Drabble, no matter what excuses he tries to find for staying at his dam. I want him at the farm. Get me?"

"Sir."

"Likewise Dick Haines. Isaac Pennington. Pity about Wilfred Wilson. I'd have liked him there, too."

Wilson reminded Wright of hospital.

"What's the news of P.C. Russell, sir?"

"Chipped his spine. He'll survive. Symptoms worse than the damage. Back at work in a month or two. They might not even have to offer him an inside job. Now for Tommy Booth. This is going to be the tricky one, Shiner. I want Tommy Booth there—in the wings, but out of sight—until the very moment I need him. With his mother. That's the toughest assignment of the lot. And it's your main job for the afternoon."

"Doesn't sound impossible, sir."

"Better bloody not be. You'll see my hand under the curtain. That's your cue to bring them on. And you'd better not muff it. Split-second timing, Shiner!"

"Shall do!" Wright said.

"And now I'm off to learn my lines. Got to be word-perfect."

He went upstairs; to bed, Wright presumed. And although Wright needed bed probably more than any other man awake on the Pennines, he did not question the priorities. Guessing from what he had heard that Ben Drabble would be as difficult a member of the cast as any, he went first down to the dam.

Snow was turning to slush underfoot, and the wheels of many vehicles had churned it up into a horrible mess. And along the lane that skirted the reservoir there was what might pass off as a comparative crowd in Carrion Clough. Landrovers and executive saloons were parked on the verge. Knots of people were leaning on the wall, looking out over the ice.

It did not look to Wright as if anything had changed since yesterday. The smooth blanket of snow was unbroken, except for the trampled tracks that led to Henshaw Rocks, and there were no signs as yet of any cracks under it.

But down by the dam itself there was heavy-footed activity. There was no visible breach in the banking, but trickles of dirty water from various elusive points in the rampart united to form a sluggish yellow stream that already extended across the road and overflowed a few feet over the banks of the Cotter Brook.

Wright could see Calverley on his motor-cycle, standing on the foot-rests in the manner of a scramble-rider, coming up the stony path that followed the valley, stopping to give information to a uniformed constable, who noted it down on a mill-board. Further down the valley a family was man-handling a handcart, rather too wide for the track, on which they had loaded the possessions of the universal refugee: bedding, chairs, quickly heaped-up treasures—a treadle sewing-machine and a bird-cage. Was Calverley warning them, or creating panic? A press photographer leaped forward, to pose the motor-cycle and the handcart in the same group.

But at the dam itself, activity was more workaday: a diesel dumper, a lorry-load of sandbags and a gang of men with shovels. Wright had no difficulty in finding Ben, who was standing in the middle of a group of workmen, protesting volubly, with a pickaxe in his hand.

Wright beckoned him aside and told him where Kenworthy wanted him to be and when.

"Impossible, Sergeant," Ben said, waving his arm in the general direction of a cement-mixer.

"Impossible or not, that's where you're going to be. Or you'll have Kenworthy to reckon with."

"What about all this, then? Who's going to do the work. And what's Kenworthy want me for, anyway?"

"Something to do with a murder," Wright said.

Ben did not like it. "He's not still on about that, is he?"

"He's not up here for the cure. Neither am I."

"I mean, he knows bloody well I didn't do it. God, he doesn't still think . . . ?"

"I know what he'll think if you're not there, mate."

Ben shifted his feet. "You'll have to ask the foreman."

And, "Yes, for God's sake get him off my neck for an hour or two," the foreman said.

Wright went to the grocer's shop, and Dick Haines was easier to handle, though by no means at ease in himself. He came unnecessarily round to the front of his counter, like a man sleep-walking."

"What's it all about, then?"

"You know as well as I do what it's all about—Margaret Halliwell."

"I *know* that. But I told Kenworthy——"

"Kenworthy knows what you told him. That's why he wants to see you."

Haines chewed his lower lip.

"Is he having Ben Drabble there too?" he asked after a pause.

"Ben will be there."

"He's got his knife into Ben, Kenworthy has. It isn't fair, Sergeant."

"Shooting Margaret Halliwell wasn't fair."

"Ben didn't shoot Margaret."

"Did *you*?" Wright hammered. He could see the sweat standing out on Haines's forehead.

"Hell fire, no!"

"Better be there, then. Otherwise you'll have Kenworthy thinking the worst of you. Two o'clock, sharp."

Wright went across to the Booths' cottage. The curtains at the window shifted slightly. Ada Booth had been watching his progress about the village.

"Have you brought it?" she asked in bitter expectation.

"Brought what?"

"My album. The superintendent promised——"

"You'll get that back this afternoon," Wright said on the spur of the moment.

"He said this morning. Faithfully."

"He wants to hang on to it for a little bit longer. It's a marvellous piece of work, your album, Mrs. Booth. Very, very helpful to us."

"I shall be lucky if I ever see it again," she said. "And I'm not taking that sitting down. That album . . ."

Tommy was sitting in his corner, saying nothing, his eyes moving from one to the other.

"I told you they'd pinch it," she said to him. "And I'm not standing for it, Mr. Wright."

"You'll get it back this afternoon, Mrs. Booth. The superintendent wants you and Tommy to come up to Moss Hill Farm."

"No!"

The witch-like scream: here was a woman with whom neither reason nor a pretence at reason would be of any avail.

"No power on earth will get me over the threshold of the Halliwells."

"What have the Halliwells ever done to you?" he asked.

"Look over your shoulder and see what the Halliwells have done for me."

Involuntarily, Wright half turned, and saw nothing, except a proprietary calendar against the greasy wallpaper, and Tommy, drooling in his chair. There must be some way of getting under her skin. Curiosity?

"I don't know all that much about what's going to happen this afternoon. But things are coming to a head. I can tell you that."

"About time, too."

"This is the pay-off for the Halliwells."

"They've had it coming to them."

"I should have thought you'd want to be in at the kill."

"Not *that* kill!"

Wright tried another tack.

"I should dress up in my Sunday best, if I were you. And has Tommy got a suit?"

"Huh!"

"This is the end of the old days," he said. "Even the dam's burst. You must be just about the oldest inhabitant of the Clough, now Thomas John's gone."

"Huh!"

"I was hoping you'd come of your own accord."

"You can't force me. You're not arresting me, are you?"

"You're right, of course. I can't force you. But I think we've got enough on Tommy to force *him*."

"You bastards," she said.

"I'll call at a quarter to two."

·22·

THE LIVING-ROOM AT Moss Hill Farm was the warmest spot in Carrion Clough. But the parlour was chilly; the coal fire had been lit too late that morning to have had much effect, and the thaw was taking all the heat from the outside walls.

And the room was packed with people, sitting self-consciously round the highly polished table. The silver tray was standing ready, with its ginger-wine bottle and elegant slender glasses. And at the head of the table sat Horncastle, the solicitor, exactly as at the reading of the will. On his right was Kenworthy, with Mrs. Booth's album and a folio of fifty-year-old newspapers in front of him. On Kenworthy's right was Judson, bulky and uncomfortable on the horsehair chair.

Edith Calverley was on the solicitor's left, her eyes ignoring everyone. Anthony was beside her, his complexion freshened up by the morning's activity. Then Emily, consciously solemn, and Pollard, in his best suit. The outsiders: Ben Drabble, Isaac Pennington and Dick Haines were crowded at the lower end of the table.

"We are here," Kenworthy said, "for the reading of a will."

Someone swallowed. Kenworthy turned to Horncastle.

"You will remember, when we were gathered on a similar occasion, I asked you about what had triggered off Thomas John Halliwell's sudden desire to make a will, what emotional upheaval . . ."

Horncastle's nod was scarcely perceptible. Kenworthy drew a fat and worn buff envelope from his inside pocket.

"1942. The date would be within a week or two of his wife's death, would it not?"

Edith Calverley stirred in her chair. Horncastle glanced at the paper and muttered agreement.

"I'd like you to read this will, Mr. Horncastle."

Reluctantly, resenting being given orders, Horncastle took the wad of papers in both hands.

"I, Thomas John Halliwell, of Moss Hill Farm, Carrion Clough, in the county of——"

"No," Kenworthy said. "Read the preamble, if you don't mind."

"This *is* the preamble, Superintendent."

"The heading then. I don't care what you call it. I'm not fussy about terminology."

Horncastle took a deliberate breath.

"Copy of the last will and testament of Thomas John Halliwell, lodged with Horncastle, Epworth and Clive, solicitors, Cotter Bridge, 18th November——"

Kenworthy interrupted.

"A copy which Margaret Halliwell had the good sense to remove to safe keeping, albeit in a dirty linen basket."

He turned to Horncastle.

"I must confess that I don't know what the outcome of this will be. Never in my career have I heard of a case of a solicitor suppressing a client's will. But I am simply asking you to read it, not to comment. Any observation you may care to make will be recorded, and may be used in evidence. You will later be charged. However, this is not the reason we are here. If you would continue to read to us, please."

Horncastle scanned a few lines of the will. Then he raised his eyes and looked into the face of each person at the table in turn. He pushed the papers back to Kenworthy.

"You read it, please," he said.

His face was proud. His eyes, for the first time since Kenworthy had met him, were tired. He was resigned to whatever retribution lay in front of him with the philosophy of an oracular old man.

"My sole intention was to save the family a good deal of unsavoury and unnecessary muck-raking," he said. Then he saw that Judson was scribbling down his words, and closed his mouth firmly. The lawyer in him was not dead.

Kenworthy picked up the will.

"I think we might skip the legal jargon," he said, looking round the table for approval. There was no reaction at all. He began to read, rapidly running over the solicitors' niceties, speaking with greater deliberation when he came to the concrete items.

" 'To Thomas Booth, my natural son, the sum of one thousand pounds——' "

Edith drew in her breath.

"That isn't true."

"Actually," Kenworthy said, "Ada Booth had two pregnancies in her younger life. The first, which led to her dismissal from an affluent household in Cotter Bridge, was terminated by a successful abortion. Paternity was never satisfactorily ascribed."

He looked hard at Horncastle, who lowered his head.

"The second attempt at abortion did not succeed."

"We shall fight this in the courts," Edith said, and looked

to Anthony for support. But he would not allow her to catch his eye.

" 'To the heirs or assignees of Caleb Wardle, of Henshaw Fold Farm, the sum of £750, being the amount by which I defrauded him on the conveyancing of land to me' — I'm afraid," Kenworthy said, "I know nothing of the heirs of Caleb Wardle."

"There aren't any," Horncastle said, without looking up.

"Well, the assignees are probably going to be a troublesome lot to find. — 'To the heirs or assignees of Abraham Drabble, the sum of £350 . . .' Not a lot, Ben. And he managed to salve his conscience without translating his sums into current values. Mind you, £350 in the 1890s was a different kettle of fish. Not worth a murder, of course, but . . ."

Ben glowered with bloodshot eyes. "I'd nothing to do with it."

"I know you hadn't. All I said was, it wasn't worth a murder. Still less in your case, Dick. Alfred Haines, Starve-acre Farm, £150. And you, Isaac, only £50. No land in your case, I think, but something to do with agricultural implements. And all the residue — that would have been after the sale of the freehold of this farm, for what that's worth — 'to my beloved granddaughter, Margaret Halliwell.' I fear there's no mention of anyone else."

"Well, that's fair enough," Bernard Pollard said after a pause, and Emily, a blotchy patch of white powder on her pink cheek, murmured agreement.

"May I see it, please?"

Anthony Calverley held out his hand for the will, looked at it intently at first, then skimmed the final paragraphs before passing it back to Kenworthy.

"The old man was shrewd," Kenworthy said. "This is dated 1942. Margaret was only a child. She hadn't even begun to housekeep for him. But he knew full well which way things were going to go. And he knew what sort of a conscience he was going to have to live with. But he hadn't quite the guts to kill it. All he could do was apply a local anaesthetic."

"None of which helps us to find the murderer," Calverley said. "It's very thoughtful of you to apply yourself so assiduously to our family affairs, and I'm sure we're all deeply appreciative. But it isn't the purpose for which they sent you up from London, is it?"

"The murderer's sitting at this table," Kenworthy said simply. "It's easy for us to say that no one would murder for paltry amounts like this. But there are people about who might have greatly over-estimated what the amounts would be. Aren't there?"

He looked round their faces: Ben Drabble, exhausted by his physical and emotional exertions at the dam; Isaac Pennington, wide-eyed and ill at ease, Bernard Pollard, drumming with his finger-tips.

"Or again," he continued, "it might have been nothing to do with money at all. It might have been vicarious passion."

Anthony Calverley held himself motionless.

"It might have been sheer jealousy, envenomed family relationships."

Edith did not even appear to be breathing.

"It could even have been an act of tragic imbecility. But actually, it was none of these things."

Kenworthy drew the large folio of newspapers towards him and opened it at a page he had marked with a folded envelope.

"It was Ada Booth who played the answer into my hands, just as soon as I realized who it was she was trying to protect when she removed a cutting from her album. If she had not done that, I wouldn't ever have known that there *was* anyone she'd want to protect."

He slewed the folio round on the table, so that Anthony could look squarely at it.

"He looks very much like his father, doesn't he? There's only one figure in this group who could be mistaken for anyone else by living in Carrion Clough today."

Anthony looked sideways at Horncastle, and nodded. Horncastle raised his eyes, and looked Kenworthy in the face.

"You knew of the existence of this," Kenworthy said, indicating the will. "You only suspected the existence of *this.*"

From his inside pocket he brought out a thin, folded quarto document, bound in brown paper.

"This is Thomas John's complete self-exoneration. This is his unembroidered account of what really happened when the gathering grounds changed hands. How you and your father, Horncastle, put up the capital and the ideas. How you invented the lies that had to be told and the rumours that had to be spread. How you had to have a couple of front men to do the buying and selling, because, of course, you wouldn't want to sully your own fingers with anything underhand. Just another case of conscience."

Horncastle felt in his waistcoat pocket for his snuff-box, poured a few grains on to the back of his hand, and applied it to each of his nostrils.

"You're a proud old man, Horncastle. You are in the evening of your days. You have got, what, five, ten years to live? You would not want to spend them under the opprobrium of a community that used to regard you as something little lower than the gods. You knew there was a copy of the will. You'd a pretty good idea that Thomas John would also have put pen to paper on his own account. But when you came up to Moss Hill Farm that afternoon, anything like murder was far from your mind. What had you intended to do? See the family, appeal to Anthony Calverley's dislike of adverse publicity, play up to his mother's ruthless respectability?"

Horncastle betrayed no reaction.

"With their connivance, you could have suppressed these documents, though it must have crossed your mind that it would be by no means so easy to silence Margaret. Unfortunately for her, you happened into the farmyard at the very moment when she charged out of the house. You had to see her first, because you guessed that only she knew about these papers—and where they were. You followed her to the tree. You made your proposition. And she flew at you like a wild cat, suddenly whipped the gun out of the hole in the tree and ordered you off the premises. You grappled with her, took it from her. Then you heard the door of the farm open and shut. Margaret was making an unholy row. You panicked—and fired." Judson's heavy breathing was the only sound at the table.

"Pure supposition," Horncastle said.

"I will admit that I have had to develop a hypothesis. And I am still not sure how you managed your comings and goings. We shall question your chauffeur, of course, though I expect he will do his best to remain loyal to you. And I don't expect it was to Carrion Clough you had him drive you. You know the byways pretty well, and you're a tough old bird, even in the snow."

Horncastle permitted himself a thin smile.

"Highly ingenious, Superintendent. But you will be hard put to it to show that I was anywhere near Carrion Clough on the afternoon in question."

Kenworthy stood up, left the table and went to the window, where he thrust his hand between the curtain and the pane. From within the doorway of one of the outhouses, Shiner Wright saw the signal. The door opened, and he ushered Tommy Booth into the room.

Tommy was smiling, with especial warmth for Horncastle.

"Good afternoon, Mr. Shelmerdine," he said.